Shadow Lily

G.J. Walker-Smith

Shadow Lily

Print Edition

© 2016 G.J. Walker-Smith

Other Books by G.J Walker-Smith
Saving Wishes (Book One, The Wishes Series)
Second Hearts (Book Two, The Wishes Series)
Sand Jewels (Book 2.5, The Wishes Series)
Storm Shells (Book Three, The Wishes Series)
Secret North (Book Four, The Wishes Series)
Silver Dawn (Book 4.5, The Wishes Series)
Star Promise (Book Five, The Wishes Series)
Shiloh (Book Six, The Wishes Series)
Stone Roses (Book Seven, The Wishes Series)

Contact the author:
https://www.facebook.com/gjwalkersmith
gjwalkersmith@gmail.com
gjwalkersmith.com

For everyone who believes

CONTENTS

VITRIOL 1

NEW YORK MINUTE 31

THE MAGIC WAGON 37

A SHOT IN THE DARK 48

ROOKIE MISTAKE 56

COOL KIDS 67

GAELIC BLOOD 80

LOVELY AND THRILLED 105

All BARK AND NO BITE 124

SUSHI LEVEL BEAUTIFUL 131

FALLING SHORT 137

EMPIRE OF DIRT 147

CONSTRUCTIVE EDITING 161

FANFARE 191

1.VITRIOL

Lily

The Best Salon in The Cove is loud, even when there's no one there. When my sister decided to tone down the lime green décor in favour of something more chic, her husband spent an entire weekend painting the walls a frightful shade of yellow called Disco Lemon.

Predictably, Jasmine was thrilled with the result. "Oh, Wade," she beamed. "It's as if a million sunsets have exploded in here!"

That one statement summed up my sister to a T. She was excessive, over the top and out of touch – and it had taken me far too long to figure it out.

My formative years were spent idolising her. I'd grown up thinking she was cutting edge and fashion forward, but over time I came to realise she was just as backward as a small town girl could be.

Years of my life were wasted following Jasmine's airhead ways, and I used to dress like a glitzed-up hooker because of it. Dyeing my blonde hair brown and ditching the callgirl outfits took care of my fashion crimes, but growing a backbone and completely breaking free of her was taking much longer.

Smartening myself up was also a part of operation anti-airhead. I started with my vocabulary, making it my mission to learn a new word every day.

Today's word was vitriol. According to the app on my phone, it means abusive or venomous language used to express bitter, deep-seated ill will.

It wasn't a word I was likely to forget in a hurry, mainly because it came with a visual demonstration. Like a trapped rat, I was caught in Jasmine's salon on the receiving end of one of the nastiest tantrums I could remember.

And I'd brought it all on myself.

"You can't quit working here!" she screamed. "You need this job!"

She was wrong. What I needed to do was stick to my guns and make her accept that I was done being her salon lackey.

"I'm sure you'll manage without me," I muttered. "All I do is sweep hair and make coffee anyway."

"Well, I'm not doing it!" she screeched. "That's always been your job."

"Not anymore." I shrugged. "Maybe Wade could help you."

With a look of pure acid on her face, she looked me up and down. "Who's going to hire you, Lily?" she asked. "You're not qualified to do anything else."

"I'm not looking for another job," I told her, standing tall. "I'm going to concentrate on my own business."

"What business?" she barked. "Being an idiot isn't a business."

Jasmine might not have been cutting edge, but she was still cutting. When things didn't go her way she resorted to nasty insults, and I was hopeless at fighting back. Perhaps that's why I reduced my lifelong dream to dirt by explaining it badly. "I'm going to make clothes for dogs."

Jasmine let out a humourless, condescending laugh. "That's the most ridiculous thing I've ever heard. You're an idiot."

"I have it all worked out," I said, ignoring her. "Pawesome Designs will be a huge success."

Jasmine grabbed a dustpan and broom off the counter and thrust it at me. "Sewing outfits for Nancy doesn't suddenly make you a designer, Lil." She pointed at the pile of hair clippings on the floor. "Stick with what you do best."

Designing clothes for pets is what I did best. Nancy, our Pomeranian pooch, had been cursed with a bad case of eczema since puppyhood. Her incessant itching left ugly bald spots that no ointment or pill could cure. Crafting a few cute outfits was designed to pretty her up and give her a confidence boost, but over time, I realised the boost in confidence was all mine.

Nancy had an outfit for every occasion – and I designed and handmade all of them. I wasn't Lily Tate, salon lackey. I was a pet couturier, and I was damned good at it.

"It's a sound business idea, Jasmine." I thumped the dustpan down on the counter. "I have more than enough clients to keep me going."

That was a lie. To date, Nancy was my only customer, and she wasn't great when it came to paying for my services.

Jasmine flicked her hair off her shoulder, looking as superior as ever. "So you think you're some kind of bigshot now?"

"No," I muttered.

I was a small shot, but I was on my way.

"If you're going to be an entrepreneur, Lil, you should at least know how to spell it."

Little did she know, her nastiness was extremely helpful. It made standing my ground a whole lot easier. I slung my handbag over my shoulder and headed for the door. "You're a bitch, Jasmine," I told her. "B-I-T-C-H."

***

My sister can hold a grudge forever, and when Wade turned up at my door a few days after our run-in, I knew I'd been banished long term.

"I'm here to discuss the custody arrangements of Nancy." He gave the lead in his hand a tug, making the poor old dog stumble forward. "I'm the mediator."

The only things more ridiculous than the Lycra bike pants he was wearing were the words he spoke. My sister and I had been successfully sharing Nancy for the past ten years without incident.

I unhooked the lead from her collar and scooped Nancy off the floor. "Nothing has changed," I insisted. "I'll drop her off at your place on Sunday."

"*You've* changed," he accused.

I playfully slapped his beefy arm. "Aw, thanks, Wade."

"It's not a good thing, Lil." He slowly shook his head. "Family is supposed to stick together – one for one and all for all."

Jasmine's decision to marry a man with a single digit IQ was immensely helpful when it came to bolstering my self-esteem. After spending a lifetime wearing an invisible dunce hat, Wade

Davis waltzed in and took the crown from me.

To most, the attraction wasn't obvious. He was easily confused, often got his words mixed up, and had biceps like tree trunks. But I knew exactly what my sister saw in him; Wade loved her unconditionally, which was far more than she deserved most of the time. He'd also do anything for her, which is why he'd turned up on my doorstep to do her bidding.

"I think you should go down to the salon and ask Jas for your job back," he suggested. "Just tell her you're sorry and move on."

"If I live to be a hundred, that will never happen," I said, inching the door closed. "And you can tell her that."

Wade stepped forward, wedging his foot in the way. "You need a real job, Lil," he insisted. "Selling dog clothes isn't a real job."

I couldn't take offense. Wade was little more than Jasmine's parrot. If anything, I should've been praising him for remembering his lines.

"Look, I don't need to defend myself to you." I pushed him in the chest sending him stumbling back onto the porch. "Go home and tell your wife that you have nothing to report."

It wasn't the first time I'd slammed a door in his face, but it was definitely the most rewarding – right up until he delivered a parting shot that made me second guess everything.

"You're on your own, Lil," he called. "Jasmine is done with you. I hope you're happy."

There was nothing to be happy about. Walking out on my job at the salon was an act of mutiny, and my sister was likely to destroy me because of it.

Nancy wasn't the only thing we shared. Trailing in Jasmine's wake meant that we also had the same friends, and on her word alone they'd drop me in a flash. Truthfully, it would be no great loss. They were carbon copies of her; catty and judgemental, which was everything I was trying to turn my back on.

The bigger worry was the influence she had over my parents. In their eyes, my brother Mitchell was an unambitious beach bum, and I was a dim scatter-brain. We were no-hopers, but Jasmine could do no wrong. She was special and acted accordingly.

Our dad did his best to stay impartial, but Mum didn't even try to hide the obvious favouritism. I shuddered to think what she'd say when she heard about our falling out. I knew she'd take my sister's side, which meant I'd left myself open for attack, and my mother wasn't one to hold back.

I couldn't dwell. If saving my soul meant cutting my mum loose too, I was prepared to do it. I deserved better, and always had done.

***

Every few months, Floss Davis hosts strange events called crystal parties. They usually involved longwinded lectures about the healing powers of gems, an overload of vegan snacks and the obligatory purchase of semi-precious trinkets that no one really wants. Attendance is mandatory, which meant my plan of laying low didn't last long.

I knew my mum and sister would be there, and

as I stepped onto Floss' front porch, my heart was thumping because of it.

Before I had a chance to knock, the front door swung open. "Lily, lovie," crowed Floss, throwing her arms wide. "Welcome."

Keen to see what I was up against, I tried to look past her, but Floss is a big woman. I couldn't see anything beyond her flowy green kaftan.

I dutifully followed her through the cluttered front room and into the kitchen, incessantly nodding as she explained the order of proceedings.

"It's such a lovely day, I thought we'd all sit outside." Floss thrust a paper plate at me. "Get yourself some food and find a chair. I'll start the presentation soon."

I looked at the massive spread laid out on the kitchen table and couldn't see a single dish that I was willing to try. "Did you cook all of this?" I asked.

"I've been cooking for days." Her warm voice was laced with pride. "Only the best for my crystal ladies."

The smile I forced was almost painful. I had no intention of being one of her crystal ladies, but judging by the sounds of shrill giggles and high-pitched conversation coming from the back patio, I was the minority.

After ordering me to load up my plate, Floss shuffled out the door to tend to her guests. I was happy to stay put and hide in the kitchen, but the peace was short-lived. Charli walked into the room, looking just as uncomfortable as I felt. "Floss told me to get some more food." She waved a paper plate at me. "I hate this vegan crap."

I looked down at the table. "That makes two of us."

"Here." She picked up a spoon, loaded it up with something that vaguely resembled potato salad and dumped it on my plate. "Try this."

"Gee, thanks."

She grinned. "Any time."

I welcomed the light-hearted banter but knew it wouldn't last long. Charli and I weren't friends. She tolerated me, and it had been that way for as long as I could remember.

"Are you here by choice or obligation?" she asked.

I shrugged. "I have no interest in rocks."

"Well, I love rocks." Charli handed me a plastic fork. "Floss' gemmology lessons drive me nuts, though."

"But you always buy things at the end of it."

"That's why we're here, Lil," she replied. "Don't let the vegan spread and bottles of cheap wine fool you. This is Floss' hard sell. She's a shrewd business woman."

For the briefest of moments, I wondered if I should've been taking notes. I was supposed to be a business woman too, but I didn't have a shrewd bone in my body.

"I could probably learn a thing or two from her."

"Maybe," she agreed. "I heard you quit your job at the salon to branch out on your own. Doggie fashion design, right?"

"Sort of," I reluctantly confirmed. "Is that really what you heard?"

The corner of her mouth lifted. "No. I heard that you had a knock-down drag-out fight with your sister. Apparently, there was glitter and sparkles flying everywhere.”

Charli wasn't renowned for gossip. If the story had reached as far as her, it was fair to assume that the whole town knew about it.

“I'm not sure if I can face this today.” I shoved a bowl of salad aside and set my plate down on the table. “I might just leave.”

“That's what you do best, Lilian,” interrupted a voice from behind. “Your sister can attest to that.”

I didn't have to turn around to know that the jibe had come from my mother. I would've recognised her caustic tone anywhere.

“Hi, Mum.” As weak as it was, the pleasantry was wasted on her. I could tell by the look on her face that she was already in attack mode.

“I suggest you get outside and apologise to Jasmine,” she demanded, pointing to the door. “Do you have any idea of the stress you've caused her this week?”

In a strange show of unity that I wasn't expecting, Charli moved closer to my side. “Perhaps this is a conversation for another day.” Her voice was quiet but firm. “Let's not ruin Floss' party.”

My mother's harsh glare shifted to Charli. "Quite right," she falsely agreed. "It's nothing to do with you anyway. It's a family matter."

Satisfied that she now had control of the room, Mum refilled her wine glass and walked out the door, leaving nothing but embarrassment behind.

"Sorry about that," I mumbled. "She's pissed."

"Grand actions cause grand reactions, Lily," Charli replied, handing me my plate. "You just have to be brave enough to stick to your guns and see it through."

I knew she was speaking from experience. Charli Décarie was a calm and reasonable adult, but Charli Blake had been a defiant brat who constantly bucked the system and raised hell. Perhaps that's why I allowed my resolve to slip in front of her.

"I'm not feeling very brave," I admitted. "They want me sweeping up hair in the salon, and the longer I hold out, the uglier it's going to get."

"Is sweeping up hair your bliss, Lil?"

"No." The word came out in a whispered growl. "I'm not the sharpest tool in the shed,

Charli, but I'm not brain dead. I have to believe there's more out there for me than that."

Charli put her hands on my shoulders, turned me around and pushed me toward the door. "Then go outside, put on a brave face and show everyone that you mean business."

***

Jasmine's circle of friends hadn't altered much since high school, and seeing them huddled in the corner as we stepped out onto the patio reminded me of recess in the schoolyard quadrangle. Most of them still had the same hairstyle, and all of them were still hanging on Jasmine's every word.

I made a beeline for the first empty chair I saw, refusing to pay any of them more than a sideward glance. Charli took a more relaxed approach, slowly wandering past as if she was holding out for an invitation to join them.

Predictably, Jasmine stopped her. "Adam's mum hasn't been to the salon for a few days," she said. "Where is she?"

"Back in New York, I expect," replied Charli.

"They left on Wednesday."

Even from a distance, Jasmine looked gutted. Fiona Décarie had singlehandedly doubled the salon's revenue over the past few weeks, and the loss of her daily visits was surely going to sting.

"Well, that's rude."

"Totally rude," Charli shot back. "I'll be sure to call her and tell her that you think she lacks manners and class."

Horrified by the notion, Jasmine gasped. Fiona Décarie was the most glamourous woman imaginable, and my sister worshipped the ground she walked on.

"I never said that!" She held up both hands. "Don't tell her that!"

Ignoring her, Charli picked up a plastic chair and headed my way. "Touchy, isn't she?" she asked, setting it down beside me.

"We all have goals," I replied. "Jasmine wants to be Fiona when she grows up."

Charli dropped her head and let out a quiet laugh, but there was no need to be discreet. Everyone's attention was on Floss, who'd taken centre stage on the step near the back door.

"Let's get started, shall we?" She clapped her hands together. "We have a lot to get through."

I managed not to groan out loud, but plenty of others weren't as polite.

If Floss was bothered by the lack of enthusiasm, it certainly didn't show. She called Charli forward and asked her to help her. "Take this, lovie," she instructed, passing her a black velvet bag. "Pick any piece you like."

It was the perfect prelude to a magic show, but it turned out to be far less interesting. Charli dutifully pulled a purple pendant from the bag, dangling it in the air by its silver chain.

"Ahh, amethyst," crowed Floss. "The beautiful purple flame with the power to transmute negativity into light."

She'd lost me already. Transmute sounded like a word Wade would make up, and no part of the crystal was flaming.

"Amethyst has been known to cure many things including insomnia and nightmares," Floss continued. "And they're on sale today for the bargain price of thirty-five dollars."

My mother piped up. "I'll take two for the twins," she said, charging her glass. "Cheynie likes purple, and Lincoln likes flames."

"Sold!" beamed Floss.

The strong start to proceedings set the pace, and within twenty minutes, the velvet bag was empty. Floss' schoolmarm crystal lecture had nothing to do with the quick sell out. Everyone just wanted to get the hell out of there.

Jasmine's crew escaped first. They grabbed their purchases, a few half bottles of champagne and made a run for the door. The older women moved slower but were just as determined to leave.

Valerie Daintree led the pack. "I'll pick my necklace up next week, Floss," she called, already half way across the lawn.

"No worries, lovie," she replied, waving her off from the front porch. "Thanks for coming."

I was next out the door but didn't make it as far as the front steps before Floss collared me. "You need to drive your mum home, Lily love," she insisted. "She's had a bit much to drink."

I turned, looking back through the open front door. Mum had Charli bailed up in the kitchen. She still had a glass of wine in her hand, but she was steady on her feet, and the conversation looked calm.

"Are you sure?" I asked. "She looks okay to me."

It was hardly a responsible attitude, but I wasn't sure I'd survive the twenty-minute drive to the vineyard with my mother.

"She's been on the sauce for hours." Her voice was stern. "She's not driving anywhere."

"Whatever," I grumbled, heading back inside. "But you can tell her."

***

Nobody tells my mother what to do, but Floss Davis had an amazing way with words. By the time we finally got her out of the house, Mum thought that getting a lift home was her idea. Floss also has a way of roping people in against their will, and for this task, Charli became the patsy when she made her the designated driver.

As my mother gathered her belongings, Charli

pulled me aside. "If I have to drive her home, you're coming too," she hissed.

"But I have my own car here." It was a weak argument that didn't fly for a second.

"I mean it, Lil," she growled. "I'm not spending a minute alone with her. She hates me."

"Fine." I picked up my purse. "But for the record, I'm pretty sure she hates me too."

Like my sister, my mum is hugely impressed by the finer things in life. As I climbed into the back seat of the Décaries' luxury white SUV, I knew she'd pass comment – and it took less than three seconds.

"My, my, my," she purred. "What a lovely vehicle, Charli. You're a fortunate girl."

Charli glanced up, frowning at me through the rear vision mirror. "Thank you," she uttered. "It's just a car."

"It's always nice to see a hard-knock girl land a good man and build a decent life." Mum ran her finger along the woodgrain trim on the dash. "You really got lucky. Good for you."

Charli wasn't stupid. Arcing up at the

monumental insult my mother had just paid her would've lowered the tone of the conversation even further, and she knew it. I saw her knuckles whiten as she tightened her grip on the steering wheel, but her reply was polite. "I count my blessings every day, Meredith."

"At least you have blessings to count," Mum ruefully replied. "I wish poor Lily could be so lucky."

Shutting down was a defence that kicked in whenever she went on the attack. It wasn't a new concept; I'd been putting up with it my whole life. I turned to the window, focusing on the outside view as I tried to ignore her.

Daylight had almost gone. The sea beyond the sweeping cliffs was inky and dark. It was an eerie setting, but nothing compared to the sinister feeling of being trapped within earshot of a hateful conversation.

"Dog clothes," Mum hissed. "Can you believe it, Charli? She's prepared to throw away a good job at the salon to make dog clothes. Where's the security in that?"

"Plenty of small businesses are successful," Charli defended. "Everyone has to start somewhere."

"Some girls can't afford to take chances like that," she snapped. "Lily hasn't got a brain in her head. Her options are limited."

Humiliation bubbled in my gut, but it wasn't painful enough for me to speak up. I nudged the back of my mother's seat with my knee, hoping that would remind her that I was present and listening to every word.

It didn't, and the torture continued.

"Back in my day, simple girls married young," she rambled. "It was the only hope they had of making something of themselves. I'm not even sure that's an option for Lily anymore."

"Mrs Tate!" Charli snapped. "You're speaking about your daughter."

"I'm just telling it how it is," she replied nonchalantly. "Lily and I have spoken about this many times, haven't we love?" Her gentle tone belied her cruel words, but for some reason, I played along.

"Yes," I agreed.

"Of course we have. That ship sailed long ago."

Charli glanced at me through the mirror again, a look of sheer pity in her eyes. "Outrageous," she sarcastically muttered. "Left on the shelf at twenty-five."

Mum let out a long sigh. "I know, but what can I do?"

I'd never felt so relieved to see the front gates of the vineyard come into view. As soon as the car rolled to a stop, I leapt out to open them.

The air felt even thicker when I got back to the car, and the three hundred metre drive to the house played out in absolute silence.

Mum said nothing to Charli as she exited, but leaned her head through the open back window to deliver a parting shot to me. "Call your sister, Lilian," she demanded. "Apologise and tell her you'll be back at work on Monday."

It had been a long time since I'd seen Charli Blake in action, but marriage and motherhood had dulled none of her chutzpah. Without saying a word, she pressed a button on the armrest of her door and wound the window up. Mum straightened up in the nick of time, which was a relief. As furious as I was, crushing her head wasn't on my agenda.

Charli didn't hang around, leaving her choking in a cloud of dust as she sped down the gravel driveway. Neither of us said a word until we reached the front gates, but as soon as the car pulled to a stop, Charli let loose. "That woman is freaking evil, Lily!"

"She can be," I dully replied.

Charli twisted in her seat, pinning me in place with a concerned frown. "Are you okay?"

I shrugged. "Why wouldn't I be? It's nothing I haven't heard before."

I got out of the car and wandered over to close the gates, feeling Charli's eyes boring a hole through the back of my head the whole time. I could only imagine what she was thinking.

At twenty-five, I was supposed to have it all together. I wasn't meant to be trying to prove my worth to the world. By now, it should've been obvious, but when I turned around and glimpsed at Charli through the windscreen, her woeful expression proved that it wasn't.

To everyone who knew me, I was poor, simple Lily Tate and my family never did anything to dispel that perception.

I turned around, focusing on the large metal sign to the left of the gate. "Tate Estate Vineyard," I read out loud in the sourest tone I could muster.

My father was immensely proud of the business he'd built over the years. My mother was prouder of the sign. It was bold, ostentatious and self-indulgent – just like her.

In a moment of pure madness, utter contempt boiled to the surface. I picked up a piece of gravel, drew back my arm and pegged it at hard as I could. It pinged off the tin sign like a bullet but did no damage. Undeterred, I tried harder, this time using a larger rock.

Charli tumbled out of the car looking absolutely appalled. "Lily, what the hell are you doing?"

"What do you care?" My voice shook, unfairly alerting her to the fact that I was close to tears. "I don't even know how you ended up in the middle of this. You shouldn't even be here."

"I do care," she insisted. "Are you okay?"

I furiously shook my head and couldn't seem to stop. "We're not friends, Charli," I reminded her. "You don't need to pretend to be nice to me."

"What are you talking about?" She threw her arms wide. "I'm not pretending anything, and for the record, you look like you could use a friend right now."

Killing my manicure, I scraped up another rock. "Well, my first choice wouldn't be you."

"Why not?" she asked, daring to smile. "I'm freaking adorable."

"Yeah," I scoffed. "As adorable as a heart attack." I threw the rock at the sign, and completely missed it. "You bullied me all through school and beyond and now you want to be friends?"

When I bent down to pick up another rock, Charli grabbed my arm. "I bullied you?" she asked incredulously. "You and your bitch sister tormented me for years."

"That's not the way I remember it."

"Then you remember it wrong."

"You used to staple me to the pinup board by my hair!" I yelled.

Her rigid posture softened as she dropped her hold on me. "I did do that," she conceded. "But I only ever retaliated. I never started it. You did awful things to me first — and you were far more dangerous than Jasmine."

There was a reason for that. My sister fought with words. She had no reason to get her hands dirty when I was there to do her bidding. The truly nasty pranks were usually committed by me. And years after the fact, it was still a hard truth to admit to.

"Face it," I muttered. "We were both arseholes."

Charli folded her arms and leaned back against the car. "For what it's worth, I'm not that girl anymore."

"How can you be so sure?"

She frowned. "Because I've worked hard to grow up and stop being an arsehole."

"So you think people can change?"

"Yes," she replied. "If they want to."

"I'm trying really hard to change my ways too, Charli." It was secret I never expected to share out loud - least of all with her. "I'm twenty-five years old, and I have no idea who I am. Pathetic, right?"

"No." Her quiet voice was flat. "I don't think it's pathetic at all."

Confiding in someone brought huge relief, even if the confidant was Charli.

"I'm better than the person people see," I told her. "I play the dumb card because it works. Bimbo worked for a long while too, but I'm over that now."

She dropped her head, laughing down at the ground. "Do you miss being a glittery airhead?"

"No," I replied. "Do you miss being a juvenile delinquent?"

"Sometimes," she admitted. "Seeing you chuck rocks at that sign makes me twitchy."

I leaned down and picked up a rock. "Have at it," I urged, holding it out to her. "You're probably a better shot than me anyway."

She shook her head, refusing to take it. "I can't," she replied. "I promised Adam I wouldn't do anything illegal while I'm pregnant."

My eyes widened. "You're having a baby?"

"Yeah." Even in the low light, her smile was bright. "Due at the end of June."

"Congratulations, Charli." I smiled. "I'm happy for you."

"Thanks, Lil. I'm happy too."

We were quiet for a moment, but it wasn't uncomfortable. I used the time to gather more rocks. Charli was obviously still on the criminal track too. "If you really want to do some damage, aim for the light," she suggested.

I looked up at the spotlight mounted on the top of the sign, weighing up my options. "Do you think I can hit it from here?"

"I could," she boasted. "At least have a crack. If you can't, I'll come back in six months and do it for you."

My technique was terrible, but by some miracle, the fourth rock I threw was a winner. The light smashed into a million pieces, raining shards of glass onto the ground. The light went out in an instant, and like the two cowardly, crooked school girls we used to be, Charli and I bolted for the car. There really wasn't any need to flee the scene, but we did – much faster than we should've considering we were on a single lane gravel road.

I felt giddy with adrenalin. "That was amazing!"

Charli glanced across at me, grinning. "Welcome to the dark side, Lily Tate."

2. New York Minute

Charli

Better than anyone, I know how deep hateful words can cut when they come from the mouth of your mother. I only endured a few months of it before cutting Olivia from my life, but I got the distinct impression that Lily had been putting up with Meredith's abominable rants for years.

After the initial euphoria of smashing the light wore off, the drive back to the Davis' was mostly silent, which was troubling. Lily seemed far too calm – almost unaffected by her mother's poor treatment of her.

When I pulled into the driveway, she finally spoke. "Thanks for the ride," she said, unclicking her seat belt. "I guess I'll see you later."

"Lil, if you ever want to talk or –"

She cut me off with a harsh reminder. "Not friends, Charli," she said, pushing open the passenger door.

"What if I want to be friends?" It was a strange question considering our history, but strange was the theme of the day.

Lily rummaged around in her bag. "Why?" she asked, finally finding her keys. "Because you feel sorry for me?"

I wasn't sure what my reasoning was, and taking too long to think about it didn't help my cause. Lily took my silence as a yes.

"I have enough fake people in my life, Charli," she said sourly. "I don't need a new fake friend."

***

Bridget had Adam wrapped around her little finger, which meant she could talk him into almost anything. I arrived home to find that she'd somehow conned him into lighting the living room fire.

January nights are notoriously cool in southern Tasmania, but I liked to make-believe that we enjoy balmy summer evenings along with the rest of the country. Cranking up the fireplace was a no-no.

"Hello, family." I dropped my bag down on the couch. "What's going on?"

The tone of my greeting should've let them both know they were in trouble, but when they turned to face me, neither of them looked the least bit contrite.

Adam grinned. "First fire of the year."

"But it's roasting in here," I complained.

I slid open the front window before joining them at the fireplace.

"It's not that warm." Adam pulled me in close and chastely kissed my cheek. "We're just having a New York minute. Mom said it's snowing there today."

"Are you feeling homesick?" I asked.

"Why would I be?" Shifting his focus from the hypnotic flames to me, he smiled. "I am home."

Bridget picked up a small piece of kindling. "I can make all this wood burn up."

The proud but maniacal edge to her voice was

reason alone to snuff the fire out.

"I told you, baby," Adam took the wood from her, "you're not to touch it."

Bridget put both hands behind her back as if she was about to be handcuffed. "I won't," she assured him. "I'll just look nicely at it."

Looking nicely at it lasted much longer than I expected. She parked her butt on the rug and refused to move, even for dinner. I'd had my fill of diva antics for the day so I didn't fight her. After enjoying a fireside picnic dinner with her heinous best mate, Treasure, we managed to get her into bed without a fuss.

***

Now that we were alone together, Adam's summer fire turned from a novel idea to a tactical move. After tucking Bridget into bed, he returned to the living room with a glass of wine and a suggestive smile.

"Not your best work, Adam," I teased, settling further into the couch. "Wooing the pregnant lady with booze and heatstroke."

"The wine is for me," he replied, setting his glass down on the coffee table. "You can just look nicely at it."

He flopped down beside me, and I took full advantage by resting my legs across his lap. It was a relaxing end to a hectic day, but my mind was still locked on drama. "Can I ask you something?"

"Of course."

"Will you answer honestly?"

The dimple on his cheek deepened as his smile grew broader. "As long as it doesn't get me killed."

"Do you think I'm a likeable person, Adam?" I asked. "To other women, I mean."

The look that flashed across his face was a strange mix of confusion and terror. "What happens if I answer wrong?"

"There is no wrong answer," I replied with a laugh. "I just want your opinion."

"I don't think you have likeability issues, Charli." In a genius move, he rubbed my feet. "I think you have trust issues. It makes it hard for people to get to know you."

I couldn't refute a single word he said. Since

Nicole Lawson stomped our friendship into the ground, I'd never been willing to try again.

"Lily is going through a rough time at the moment."

I purposefully kept details at a minimum. Adam had never had much time for Lily and giving him more information than he needed seemed like a disservice to both of them. "I reached out to her today and she shot me down. My ego is a little bruised."

"You want to be friends with Lily Tate?" The glorious foot massage came to an abrupt halt. "I didn't see that coming."

"Neither did I," I mumbled, wiggling my toes to prompt him along. "Do you think it's a dumb idea?"

"I don't think any of your ideas are dumb," he replied. "I think it's brave to put yourself out there like that."

However ambiguous his answer might've been, it brought me comfort. I might've been a social misfit who had no friends, but at least I was loved. Somehow, that made being brave a whole lot easier.

3. THE MAGIC WAGON

Lily

Seven houses stand at the top of the cliffs on Spinnaker Road, and each one has spectacular, uninterrupted ocean views. For that reason alone, it was the most sought after real estate in town.

Back in the early eighties, my grandparents built the grandest house of them all. Intricate stonework, open plan living areas and huge windows were some of the features that made it cutting edge in its day, but the sheer size of the massive six bedroom home is what made it really impressive.

My father inherited it when my grandfather passed, and for ten long years, it sat vacant. Maintaining an empty house is costly, so when I approached him six months ago with the offer of moving into it, he jumped at the chance.

I didn't care that it was now old-fashioned and kitschy. I didn't even care that it gave off a spooky vibe at night. I'd just wanted out of my parents' house.

My mother was horrified by the idea, but not because she was worried about me. Her concerns were more long term.

"This will be the end of her, John," she warned. "She'll fill it up with stinking stray cats. A few years from now she'll be known as the spinster cat lady who lives in the mansion on the cliff."

"Nonsense," snapped my father. "It could well become her family home." He winked at me then, which was a comforting gesture that reduced my mum's insult to ash.

"Well, I hate cats," she retorted. "I won't be visiting."

And she never did, which is ironic considering that I wasn't overly fond of cats either. If I did end up as an old spinster, I'd likely fill the house with dogs – and they'd all be fabulously dressed.

***

I considered the crystal party drama to be nothing more than a blip on my radar. I woke the next morning feeling more motivated than ever to make Pawesome Designs a success. Somehow, I needed to get the word out that I was open for business and gearing up to take the pet world by storm.

It sounded fabulous and strong in my head, but putting a plan into action was proving a little trickier. After an hour of sitting on the couch with a notebook at the ready to pen my brilliant business plan, I'd achieved nothing more productive than half a page of useless flower doodles.

Dejected, I moved onto phase two – coffee and fresh air.

The ocean view from the back of the house was beautiful, but when it came to watching the world pass by, I usually opted to sit on the front veranda.

The big wicker swing chair creaked as I sat down, reminding me that it was almost as old as the house and not particularly sturdy. I set it in motion anyway, kicking myself off with my feet.

With a coffee in one hand and my phone in the other, I checked out my word of the day.

"Paucity," I read out loud. "The presence of something in small or insufficient quantities or amounts."

I almost laughed out loud. I'd stumbled across a word that practically summed up my whole life.

A paucity of confidence.

A paucity of knowledge.

A paucity of person growth.

I could've come up with a hundred more, but I was distracted by a little girl on a pink bike pedalling like mad as she wobbled her way down the road.

I knew it was Bridget Décarie long before I got a good look at her. The red fairy wings on her back gave her away, and so did the giddy giggle she gave as she made a break from her parents.

Charli continued her slow stroll, but Adam yelled something in French and ran to catch up to her. Whatever he'd said must've been serious because the little pink bike skidded to a stop — right outside my house.

"Did you see me go fast, Daddy?" she asked excitedly.

As soon as she was within reach, Adam grabbed the handlebars. "I told you to stop," he chided.

"I did stop," she replied. "I stopped very fast."

He turned the bike around and pointed in the direction they'd come from. "Go back that way," he ordered. "Slowly."

"A little bit fast?"

The hope in her voice made me smile, but Adam didn't see the funny side. "Slowly, Bridget," he repeated. "Or your biking days are over. Got it?"

"Yes I have got it," she replied, sounding totally untrustworthy.

With her dad in hot pursuit, the little girl took off pedalling as if her life depended on it.

Charli was the only Décarie who wasn't in a hurry. After a quiet word with Adam as he passed, she continued her slow stroll until she reached my gate.

"Hi Lily." She sounded as apprehensive as she looked. "Can I have a quick word?"

I wanted to say no. Dealing with Charli was always awkward but after the drama of the day before, there was now an element of embarrassment too.

She'd made no secret of the fact that she was outraged by my mum's behaviour, but I resented her input. Her life was perfect, which meant she had no right to pass comment on mine – but that didn't mean I didn't owe her an apology.

"I'm sorry about yesterday," I told her. "I was rude and you didn't deserve it."

She rattled the low iron gate. "Does that mean I can come in?"

"Charli, I've been living four doors down from you for the past six months," I reminded her. "You've never visited before. Why now?"

She pushed open the gate and wandered up to the veranda. "It's not a pity visit if that's what you're thinking," she replied. "I'm having a second crack at winning you over."

As much as I fought against doing it, I couldn't help laughing. "Still working the friendship angle, huh?"

"Why wouldn't I want to be friends, Lil?" Her smile was as crafty as she was. "You have a kick-arse swing on your porch, and I want to have a turn."

I shuffled across to make room for her. "I should probably warn you, it probably won't hold both of us."

Charli tentatively sat down, and we both looked to the roof to see if the chains were holding. "So far, so good," she replied.

I dropped my head to look at her. "What are you really doing here?"

She reached into the pocket of her shorts and pulled out a small blue gift bag. "I brought you a present," she said. "It's only small, but I want you to have it."

As I upended the bag, a pink heart-shaped necklace tumbled into my palm. It might've been small, but it also looked precious and expensive.

"I can't accept this," I said, trying to hand it back to her. "It's too much."

"Relax, Lil. It's not the Crown Jewels," she replied, refusing to take it. "It's just a trinket, but it's special – possibly even magic if you need it to be."

Charli had been on the magic wagon since childhood. It was one of the things that made her weird, but it was an intriguing kind of weird that I wished I understood better.

"How so?"

"Well, it's rose quartz," she explained. "Those who believe in the magic of crystals think it has special powers." She scuffed her foot on the floor, setting the swing in motion again. "It promotes all the good stuff – sensitivity, empathy, and aids in the acceptance of change. You seem to be making a few big changes in your life. I figured you could use it."

I tangled the silver chain around my fingers, dangling the pendant in front of me. "Did you buy this yesterday?" I asked.

She shook her head. "No, I've had it for a while," she replied. "Adam gave it to me a few months ago, right before I cut ties with my mother for the last time."

"You met your mum?" The rise in my voice was unavoidable. "When?"

The mystery of how Charli Blake came to be had been a topic of whispered conversation around town for years. As far as I knew, she'd never known her mother, and it was a shock to hear otherwise.

"I'll tell you the whole story if you want to hear it," she offered. "It's not pretty, but it's true."

I learned more about Charli in the next ten minutes than I had in the whole twenty-something years that I'd known her. As it turns out, the tough, aloof, untouchable girl with the nasty attitude and sharp tongue wasn't indestructible.

She'd suffered an emotional beating at the hands of her long lost mother and then run home to Pipers Cove to recover from it.

"I tried so hard to make it work." Her quiet voice was laced with frustration. "But in the end, I had to accept that sometimes it's best just to let things go. Cutting her out of my life was the only choice I had."

"She was really that awful?"

"A whole bag of nasty, Lily," she confirmed with an awkward smile. "I hope I never see her again."

The sudden push to be friends didn't seem so odd anymore. Witnessing my mum's mean rant probably reminded her of all the times she'd dealt with her own drama. Charli didn't necessarily feel sorry for me; she understood what I was going through, and recognised that making a permanent break was impossibly hard.

"I'm trying to be stronger when it comes to dealing with Jasmine and my mum." I dropped the necklace back into the bag and slipped it into my pocket. "But it's harder than I expected it to be."

Charli's warm smile hit me hard. "Rome wasn't built in a day, Lil. It's a process."

***

The next few hours flew by. The more we talked, the more I realised that I really didn't know Charli well. Her candidness surprised me, and I tried hard to return the favour. When she asked about my plans for Pawesome Designs, I laid out my entire business plan.

"It's sketchy, at best," I admitted. "But I'm just going to fake it until I make it."

"I'm very familiar with that plan," she replied. "Are you just going to make the clothes to order?"

I slowly shook my head. "It's probably going to be a while before I have to sew a stitch."

Clearly confused, she asked what I meant.

I put my feet on the floor, jolting the swing to a stop. "Come inside and I'll show you."

4. A SHOT IN THE DARK

Charli

A weird sense of Déjà vu hit me as I followed Lily into the house. I recalled attending a birthday party years ago when her grandparents lived there. I wondered if she remembered it too.

"Jasmine's seventh birthday," she confirmed. "Mum organised that weird clown from Sorell who scared everybody, remember?"

"Yes," I replied, laughing. "He did magic tricks."

Lily glanced back at me but didn't slow her walk. "He accidentally set fire to the decorations. That was magic."

"I think he was drunk."

"Totally wasted," she agreed, giggling. "Good times."

For a quick moment, I wondered how things might've been different if we'd all managed to stay as innocent and sweet as we were back then. We'd all changed, and not entirely for the better.

One thing that hadn't changed was Grandpa Tate's house. It was stuck in an eighties time warp, overloaded with mission brown cabinetry and burnt orange tiles, but the place was pristine. Adam would've called it a renovator's delight, and I made a mental note never to let him see it.

Lily led me through the huge house to one of the back bedrooms. "This is where I keep all of my stock," she said, making a grab for the door handle. "Don't be weirded out by it."

I tried not to be, but when the door swung open, I came face-to-face with the biggest collection of doggie apparel in the southern hemisphere. I took a few steps inside, trying to keep my expression straight as I took it all in. Lily's organisational skills were epic. Boxes were stacked upon boxes, and each one was labelled according to size and occasion. "There must be a thousand outfits in here," I choked.

"I've been making them for ten years, Charli," she said sheepishly. "Nancy wears some of them, but most have never been worn."

We'd passed by Nancy on the way through the living room. The ugly little pooch was fast asleep on the couch with her tongue hanging out, trussed up in a sequined hoodie. After pulling a small tuxedo out of an open box, I realised that must've been her casual weekend wear.

"How on earth are you to going shift this stuff?"

"Online, hopefully. I have a website." She shrugged. "It had four hits yesterday, but I haven't sold anything yet."

My eyes drifted back to the boxes. "What made you decide to finally go into business?"

I couldn't fathom what had taken her so long. She could've been selling her wares years ago.

Lily folded her arms and leaned against the doorframe. It was a casual gesture that didn't match the worry in her voice. "I needed a nest egg," she replied. "Working at the salon wasn't exactly lucrative. It took me years to build up some savings to fall back on."

The more she explained her plans, the more I realised that Lily wasn't going in blindly. Years of planning and thought had gone into her Pawesome Designs venture.

"I'm going to have to live on my savings until I start generating income," she told me. "I figure I've got about three months to make that happen before I'm broke and begging Jasmine for my job back."

For her sake, I desperately hoped it wouldn't come to that, but a room full of stock and four hits on her website wasn't going to cut it. I just couldn't bring myself to say it out loud.

"You'll figure it out," I assured her. "I'll help you if you want me to."

"You don't have to do that, Charli."

"Look, Bridget starts school in a few weeks, Adam's busy tearing up boats and I have no friends," I teased. "What else am I going to do?"

She motioned toward my belly with a nod. "But you're pregnant."

"Sitting around and waiting to lose sight of my feet isn't a full-time job, Lil," I replied. "I have plenty of free time on my hands."

"Do you really think I can do this?"

I thought very carefully before speaking. The question hadn't come from the dizzy Lily Tate I'd known and didn't love. It came from a girl I barely knew who was taking a massive shot in the dark at fulfilling a lifelong dream. She had to know I admired her for it.

"Did you meet my father-in-law while he was here?" She shook her head, telling me no. "He's a hard arse, but one of the smartest people I know. He once told me that nothing worth having comes easy – not love, not success, not respect. We have to work hard for it." I grabbed the doggie tuxedo out of the box and held it out to her. "This room holds ten years of hard work. By my reckoning, you're already doing it."

***

Ryan had been telling me for years that I possessed zero talent when it came to business management, and I was beginning to think he was right. I had no clue how to get Pawesome Designs off the ground, and Lily wasn't exactly bursting with ideas either.

"Maybe we should revamp the website," she finally suggested.

"Great idea." I gave her two thumbs up. "How do we do that?"

"I don't know," she replied. "But I guess logging onto the computer would be a good start."

Abandoning the boxes, we headed to the dining room. The huge open space could've accommodated a suite as grand as the Décaries' sixteen seater monstrosity, but Lily's design ideas were a little less ostentatious.

A cheap plastic outdoor table and chairs stood in the middle of the room. It was a practical solution for a single girl on a budget, but Lily had taken it to the next level. A blue and white striped beach umbrella was speared through the centre of the table.

"It came with the table," she explained. "It seemed a shame to waste it."

I looked up at the vaulted ceiling, noticing that the umbrella cleared it with at least ten feet to spare. It may well have been the most fabulous thing I'd ever seen, but it wasn't without its problems. "Lil, didn't anyone ever tell you that it's bad luck to open an umbrella inside?"

She sat down at the table and lifted the lid on her laptop. "That's why I opened it outside and then brought it in," she replied. "I might be an idiot, but I'm a resourceful idiot."

"Touché, Lily Tate. Touché."

***

I sat on the plastic chair until my butt went numb, and my mind wasn't faring much better. We tossed around a million ideas for improving the website, but there was only one that excited me – a gallery of professional photos using puppy models to showcase Lily's designs.

"We can make a whole production of it," I told her. "As elaborate as you want it to be."

Despite my enthusiasm, she didn't look convinced. "It sounds expensive," she said cautiously. "I haven't budgeted for any of this."

Fearing a meltdown was imminent, I quickly

elaborated. "It won't cost you a cent," I assured her. "I'm a photographer, and Gabi is an artist. I'm sure she could take care of the set design."

Her blue eyes widened. "You'd do that for me?"

"Of course," I replied, pushing my chair back. "It'll be fun."

"What do you need me to do?"

"Just come up with a theme." Raising my arms, I stretched out my stiff body. "If you've got some spare time tomorrow, we can pitch the idea to Gabi."

Lily followed me to the front door. "I would love that," she replied. "Is there anything else you need?"

As I got to the door, I turned back to face her. "Dogs," I said with a smile. "Lots and lots of photogenic, happy dogs."

5. ROOKIE MISTAKE

Lily

Sharing custody of Nancy with my sister meant that all decisions regarding her care had to be run past her, and Jasmine wasn't always amenable.

"Two hundred and sixty bucks for a course of injections that might not work?" I held the phone away from my ear, and she still sounded loud. "That's ridiculous!"

Nancy was an old dog, and arthritis was beginning to cripple her. The cold weather was particularly debilitating, and I constantly worried that the coming winter would be her last.

Jasmine's complaints about the cost of treatment were nothing more than puffing. She was just as concerned about our treasured old dog as I was, which was proven when she demanded to be at her next vet appointment.

"If I'm paying for half the treatment, I might as well be there to see it," she snapped.

"Great." My cheerful tone was purely designed to aggravate. "It's tomorrow morning at nine."

"Why so freaking early?"

"Because I have some important business to attend to in the afternoon."

Playing Charli's sidekick while she begged Gabrielle to take part in our photoshoot wasn't exactly important, but Jasmine didn't need to know that.

"What business?" she snapped. "No one does business on a Sunday."

"The vet does," I replied, gearing up to end the call. "I'll see you tomorrow."

Hanging up on her felt wonderful, but baiting her had felt even better. The chokehold she'd always had on me was already starting to slip, and judging by the slew of catty text messages I received throughout the rest of the day, Jasmine must've realised it too.

***

We met in the car park of the vet clinic early the next morning. Jasmine's mood was already pissy, which was exactly what I was expecting.

"He better be running on time," she warned, slamming the door of the minivan. "Lincoln's got footy training at ten."

"You didn't have to come," I replied, handing Nancy to her. "I can handle it."

"I *did* have to come," she retorted, craning her neck as Nancy licked her face. "That greedy city vet is trying to get one over on us, and I'm not going to let it happen."

Paying your dues in a country town is a long process. Despite the fact that Noah Holt had been in Pipers Cove for nearly three months, he was still known as the city vet, and probably would be for years.

Jasmine hadn't always thought ill of him. When he first arrived in town, she worked hard to pull him into her social fold, bombarding him with everything from dinner invitations to offers of discount haircuts – and he declined every one of them. The final straw came when he knocked back a coveted spot on her husband's fitness crew.

"It's the most elite fitness organisation in town," boasted Wade.

Despite the hard sell, a group of sweaty blokes running around the local park was about as prestigious as a root canal. Understandably, Noah wasn't interested, and the Davis' took it personally.

"He's a stuck up snob," declared Jasmine.

"He's not a real doctor either," added Wade. "He only works on animals."

It was a ludicrous statement, but they'd made up their minds. Noah Holt was not Team Davis material.

As soon as we walked through the door, I realised that we must've snagged the first appointment of the day. The waiting room was empty, and the front desk was unattended.

Jasmine sat down beside me, nursing Nancy on her lap. "Business must be slow."

I turned my head in time to catch her sly smirk.

"Where is he, anyway?" she asked. The door of the examination room was open a few inches.

Jasmine leaned, trying to see inside, and then answered her own question. "He's probably holed up in his office counting all his money."

When my sister's mean side kicked in, it really kicked in. Not one word out of her mouth that morning had been pleasant, which meant talking to her was a complete waste of my time. Ignoring her as best I could, I sat in silence until Noah finally walked out of his office.

"Sorry about the wait," he said. "We're a bit short-staffed this morning."

Jasmine glanced at the empty front desk. "Where's Susie?"

Noah grinned. "She's busy out the back," he replied. "Counting all my money."

A normal person would've been mortified that he'd overheard her rude comment, but Jasmine wasn't normal. She scooped Nancy up and jumped to her feet. "Let's just get this over with, shall we?"

I dropped my head, directing my laugh at the floor, which infuriated her even more. She turned around and told me to pull myself together. "You're embarrassing yourself," she chided.

The vet clinic didn't have the depressing vibe of a doctor's surgery. It was still clinical and white, but it was essentially a happy place that smelt like disinfectant and hay.

With the exception of a row of cupboards, a big stainless steel examination table and a sink in the corner, Noah's office was bare, but the pinup board of pet pictures that took up the whole far wall brightened the space immensely.

The presence of Noah enhanced the place too. He was young, handsome and kind to animals. And if those attributes didn't make him perfect, his veterinary degree did.

I wasn't the only one who got a bit hot under the collar when I saw him. Nancy had a skip in her step too. When Noah took her from Jasmine and set her down on the table, she excitedly bounced around as if she didn't have an arthritic bone in her body.

Carefully, he checked her over. "How has she been?" he asked.

"Fine," replied Jasmine.

Frowning at her, I gave a more honest reply. "Old and slow," I said. "Nights are the worst."

"The injections should help," he explained, glancing up at me. "Eighty percent of pets respond quickly after the first dose."

Jasmine's hands moved to her hips. "Those aren't good odds considering you're charging us a mint for them, Noah."

He shrugged. "I'm happy to do a thirty-day account for you."

Considering that the animosity between them was mutual, it was a remarkably generous offer, but my sister didn't agree.

"How about a discount instead?"

As audacious as her request was, Noah didn't bat an eyelid. "I've got an idea," he said sarcastically. "How about a thirty-day account?"

"Sixty," she countered.

Jasmine was much easier to deal with when she was feeling victorious and superior. Perhaps Noah realised it too. He agreed straight away.

"Excellent," she quipped, hitching her handbag higher onto her shoulder. "My work here is done."

"Wait," I called as she got to the door. "Where are you going?"

Jasmine turned back, screwing up her nose. "I hate needles," she replied. "Just bring her out to the car when you're done." She made a grab for the handle. "Oh, and Lil," she added, turning around again. "Don't let him talk you into anything else. We can't afford it – especially you." She looked me up and down. "You have no job, remember?"

Jasmine's ability to make me look foolish in front of others was pure artistry, but my skills when it came to ignoring her were better.

"Just go," I muttered. "I'll bring Nancy out soon."

As soon as the door clicked closed, I felt free to breathe again. Even Nancy looked more relaxed. Noah prepared a syringe, whispered a few sweet words into her furry ear and then administered the shot.

She didn't even flinch, but I wobbled a bit. "Do you think that hurts her?" I asked.

"I think her aching joints hurt her more," he replied, handing the pooch a treat. "An injection is a quick pinch." He lowered Nancy to the floor and headed for the sink. "But arthritis is a constant throbbing pain – probably similar to being locked in a room with your sister."

The smile he flashed as he turned around was almost as sly as his comment.

"I can call her back in here, you know," I teased. "Maybe let her know that I've negotiated a new ninety-day account."

Noah slowly stepped toward me, drying his hands with paper towel. "Do that," he said in a deliciously low tone. "And then maybe I'll let her know that you're ready to resume salon duties."

"You wouldn't dare."

He tossed the paper towel into the bin and stepped closer, pressing his whole body against me. "I might," he threatened. "You should never trust a city vet."

I did trust him. I also really liked him, which was terrifying. Historically, handsome, smart, city boys didn't land in the Cove very often, and when they did, they didn't pursue me.

Something about Noah Holt was different. He saw more in me than most people did, including my family. He listened when I spoke, encouraged me when I needed it, and took very good care of my decrepit old dog.

He was perfect, but I was a work in progress, which meant he was likely to disappear in a puff of smoke at any given moment. For that reason alone, my budding romance with the city vet was a secret I wasn't willing to share.

"I need your help with something," he murmured.

The tone of his voice suggested it was going to be something lovely, but the words didn't match. He had a house call to make that evening and wanted me to tag along.

I linked my arms around his neck. "What for?"

"A few reasons." He dropped his head, lightly pressing his lips against mine. "When you're with me, I get to kiss you any time I want to."

"That's true," I whispered.

"I also need your professional help."

I huffed out a sharp laugh. "I don't have a profession."

Breaking the hold I had on him, Noah grabbed

a pen from his shirt pocket. He took my hand and scrawled an address on my palm. "Can you meet me here at seven?"

"You are such a city slicker," I teased. "There are eleven streets in this town. You didn't have to write it down."

He slipped the pen back into his pocket. "Rookie mistake," he replied, smiling. "So you'll be there?"

I cocked my head, reading the messy doctor writing on my hand. I knew the street well, of course, but couldn't place the house at number nine. "I'll be there," I assured him. "I'll just have to cancel my other hot date."

His hand wrapped around my hip. "Do that," he said, pulling me forward. "And I'll make it up to you with dinner and a movie."

His offer was another rookie mistake. The nearest movie theatre was eighty kilometres away, but I let it go. Nancy had begun scratching at the door, which meant we had thirty seconds left together before she completely ruined the moment by peeing on the floor.

6. COOL KIDS

Charli

My would-be stepmother is no pushover. She's also a major control freak so asking her to take part in our photoshoot meant giving her total creative licence. I spent the drive out to Alex and Gabi's reassuring Lily that surrendering to her bossy ways was for the best.

"Gabrielle will turn it into a classy affair." I glanced across at her. "She has that whole French chic thing going on."

At best, it sounded silly. Nothing about the combination of dogs, costumes and photoshoots sounded classy, but Bridget thought otherwise. She piped up from the backseat. "My daddy is French," she said proudly. "He has French cheeks too."

Lily directed her quiet giggle at the window, but Bridget caught on. She let out a cackle of her own – and that sweet little sound set the mood for the rest of the journey.

It was far too soon to claim that Lily and I were friends, but we'd made serious headway in the past few days. The drama that had tainted every interaction we'd had in the past twenty years was gone, replaced by easy conversation and a mutual desire to play nice.

I couldn't deny that it was a strange turn of events, but Alex seemed to have trouble processing it. While Bridget showed Lily around the garden, he cornered me on the veranda. "What's the deal, Charli?" he asked, bouncing Jack on his hip. "You haven't invited Lily over since kindergarten."

"There is no deal," I insisted. "I'm just testing out the friendship waters."

"With Lily Tate?" he asked, eyes wide. "Why?"

He made it seem like the most ridiculous idea on earth, and a week ago, I might've agreed with him.

"As it turns out, we're not that different, Alex."

I reached, running my fingers through my brother's curls. "Flawed, but trying to do better."

"You're not –"

"Face facts, Dad," I interrupted. "Jack is the cool one. He's going to grow up having a million friends and really awesome hair."

His brown eyes crinkled at the edges as he smiled. "And you're not cool?"

"I haven't been cool once in my whole life."

"How could that be?" he asked laughing. "You're my kid. You were born awesome."

I rested my elbows on the railing and gazed down into the garden. Lily was standing at the edge of the bogan golf platform, trying to look interested as Bridget lined up her shot.

"My best friend is four-years-old." I made it sound like I was admitting to something terrible. "And in a few short weeks, she's going to dump me for the bright lights of pre-primary."

When Alex moved to stand beside me, Jack grabbed a handful of my hair. "She's still going to need you, Charli."

"I know that," I replied, loosening Jack's iron

grip. "But it's time I found some new friends."

Without warning, the screen door burst open, and Gabrielle stepped outside. "I think that's a wonderful idea," she said, taking the baby from Alex. "Getting out of your comfort zone will be good for you, Charli."

I didn't care that she'd probably been hanging on every word. The news that I was unpopular and antisocial wasn't new. I'd always been that way, and she knew it.

"How about your comfort zone, Gabs?" I asked. "Do you feel like stepping out of it for a minute? Lily and I have a proposition for you."

She said no, but I could tell by the look on her face that she was desperate for more information. I didn't make her wait long, explaining the whole plan in a few messy sentences.

"We want you to design the set," I told her. "It's got to look classy."

"Dogs wearing ball gowns?" Her green eyes were wide. "How can I make that classy?"

The almighty crack of a golf ball made us all turn our heads in Bridget's direction.

"That girl has one hell of a swing," Alex proudly noted. "She couldn't do that in Central Park."

"Not without getting arrested, no," I agreed. "Can we get back to the topic at hand, please?"

"You can," he said, stepping off the porch. "But I'd rather play golf with my grandbaby."

I turned my attention back to Gabrielle. "So?" I asked. "Will you do it?"

"Ball gowns on dogs, Charli," she repeated, looking aghast. "There is no class to be found."

I was so focused on talking her around that I hadn't noticed that Lily was now within earshot.

"I know it sounds weird, Gabi," she said, slowly making her way up the steps. "That's why I brought my sketchpad with me." She pulled a large notebook from her bag and held it out to her. "Hopefully it'll give you a better idea of what I do."

Gabrielle could sniff out lead pencils a mile away. Without uttering another word, she offloaded her baby into my arms and took the sketchpad from her.

From the corner of my eye, I could see that nerves were already getting the better of Lily. She nervously wrung her hands together, undoubtedly waiting for the Parisienne to shoot her artistic abilities to pieces.

I was nervous too. Gabrielle wasn't one to hold back when it came to giving her honest opinion. A bad critique was likely to send Lily over the edge, and I wasn't sure what that would entail.

Gabi aimlessly wandered around the porch, thumbing through pages, focusing longer on some than others. By the time she finally spoke, Lily looked close to tears.

"Where did you learn to draw like this?" she asked.

Lily shrugged. "I've always liked to draw," she replied. "It made up for the fact that my reading and writing skills sucked."

Gabrielle held the notebook to her chest, showcasing an amazing drawing of a dog kitted out in a tutu and tiara. "This is fabulous," she praised. "You have an extraordinary talent."

"Yes, she bloody does," I agreed, stepping closer to take a better look. "Who else knows you can draw like this?"

The look on Lily's face was all wrong. She should've looked proud or smug or both. Instead, she looked embarrassed. "No one," she replied. "They're just drawings."

Gabi tapped the notebook with her palm. "This is a gift," she told her. "And if your creations are half as good as your vision, you deserve huge success."

"So you'll do it?" I asked, bouncing Jack on my hip.

Her beauty queen smile was huge. "It would be my pleasure."

***

The hardware store and Bridget were not a good match, so when Alex offered to watch her for the afternoon while Lily and I took care of Gabrielle's short shopping list, I was grateful.

"Tell Norm that you want white canvas drop sheets," she instructed. "Not the plastic ones Adam uses; they have to be canvas."

"Okay," I replied, slipping her list into my pocket.

"White, Charli," she repeated. "They must be white."

She was still calling out instructions as we drove away, which was actually a good sign. When Gabrielle Décarie is in, she's all in.

***

Nothing can be done on the sly in a small town, even at three o'clock on a Sunday afternoon. As soon as I pulled into the angled parking bay in front of the hardware store, our quick and easy shopping trip suddenly became complicated.

Every shop in town was located on the main street, and The Best Salon in the Cove was opposite the hardware store. It was closed on Sundays, but today it was a hive of activity.

Through the rear vision mirror, I had a perfect view of Wade and Jasmine cleaning the front windows. Lincoln and Cheynie were running amok, chasing each other along the footpath with buckets on their heads, and little Lachlan sat in his pram chewing on a sponge.

"Probably not the best chew toy for a baby," I

said, thinking out loud.

Lily twisted the knob on her door, angling the side mirror to get a better view. "I've seen him eat worse," she muttered.

"Maybe they haven't seen us," I said hopefully.

"We're hardly incognito, Charli." Lily flapped her hands around. "If you ever decide to take up robbing banks, don't do it in this car."

I let out a soft giggle. "Just so you know, I didn't choose this wanky car."

"And just so you know," she retorted, "this car has wanker written all over it."

We were both giggling now, but there was nothing funny about the situation. Already half way across the street, Jasmine was closing in on us, which was a sure-fire sign that things were about to get ugly.

A few seconds later, she tapped on the passenger side window. In a less than generous move, Lily wound it down half way.

"This is the important business you had to take care of today?" snapped Jasmine.

"Pretty much," replied Lily.

Jasmine glowered at me. "And why are you here?" she asked. "You don't even like Lily."

I bit back quickly. "Don't tell me who I like."

She turned her attention back to her sister, adopting a calm tone that was faker than her hair colour. "We could really use your help at the salon, Lil," she said sweetly. "Just cleaning windows and stuff."

It was a fascinating display. I'd seen Jasmine's jealous streak surface a million times, but it never involved her sister. I sat in stunned silence as she tried to woo Lily back.

"I can't, Jasmine." Her tone was quiet but strong. "I'm busy."

I couldn't believe that Jasmine's sucking lemon expression was intentional. From what I could tell, she was doing her level best not to explode.

"Another time then," she said, forcing a smile.

Lily got out of the car, and I followed suit. Without saying another word, we headed into the hardware store. It would've been a clean getaway, if not for the fact that Jasmine followed us inside.

Lily spun around. "What are you doing?" she

hissed. "Following us?"

"Hardly," she replied, looking outraged. "I need some more cleaning supplies."

"What do you need, love?" asked Norm, appearing out of nowhere.

Jasmine didn't miss a beat. "Window cleaner," she replied. "And some sponges, please. Lachlan chewed the other ones."

Norm let out a loud guffaw that didn't stop until he reached the end of the aisle. When he returned a minute later, he handed Jasmine the goods she'd asked for. That should've been her cue to leave, but predictably, she didn't budge.

"Was there something else?" Norm asked, frowning at her.

"No, that's it," she replied, setting her wares down on the counter.

Clearly baffled, he turned to me. "How about you, Charli?"

I took the list out of my pocket and read it out loud. "Nine feet by twelve feet white drop sheets — four of them, please."

"Not the plastic ones," interjected Lily. "We

need canvas ones."

"Are you sure?" Norm asked me. "Adam always get the plastic ones."

"They're not for Adam," I replied. "They're for us."

Even before I looked at her, I knew that Jasmine was in a bad way. Curiosity and an acute lack of information had just about done her in.

"Anything else?" he asked.

Knowing full well that there was nothing else written on it, I looked at the list in my hand. "Yes," I replied, thinking on my feet. "A five-metre extension lead, a sixty-watt light globe and some screws."

Norm's frown intensified. "What sort of screws?"

I'd always maintained that I spent too much time in Adam's shed, and the next words out of my mouth proved it. "Countersunk rib head screws," I rambled.

Lily looked at me as if I'd lost my mind, but as soon as she leaned across and read the list in my hand, her whole expression changed. There was a game in play, and now she knew it.

Norm disappeared to get our unwanted goodies, and as soon as he was out of earshot, Jasmine pounced.

"What the hell are you up to?" She grabbed Lily by the arm and pulled her close to her side.

For some reason, I was fighting the urge to pull her back.

"It's nothing to do with you, Jasmine," she spat. "My business is my business."

"Well, what's it got to do with Charli?" Totally frustrated, she slapped both hands on her sides. "You hate each other."

I was eager to hear her reply, but it never came. Norm returned, holding up two packets of screws. "Seventy-five or a hundred millimetres?" he asked.

Lily's eyes never left Jasmine. "Both, please," she replied. "I'm building something huge."

7. GAELIC BLOOD

Lily

A smarter girl probably would've researched who lived at number nine Swift Street before agreeing to a meeting there at dusk. But I wasn't renowned for being smart. As soon as I pulled up in front of the house, I recognised it in an instant.

Using nothing more than the power of his brooding good looks and wandering hands, the city slicker vet had lured me to crazy Edna Wilson's house.

To anyone who grew up in the Cove, Edna was the scariest lady in existence. Some thought she was a witch, and others claimed she was psychic, but in my opinion, she was just a crazy old woman who got a kick out of scaring small children.

Surprisingly, her run down old house didn't

seem quite so menacing at night. The lights were on, casting a yellow glow that almost made the place seem inviting.

The string of fairy lights draped around the dead oak tree in the front yard was a nice touch too, but on the off chance it was a signal beacon for demons I locked my doors and opted to stay in the car until Noah arrived.

Thankfully, he didn't keep me waiting long, pulling in behind me just a few minutes later.

As I walked the short distance to his car, the driver's side door swung open.

"You made it." He reached into the backseat and grabbed his bag. "I was worried you might get lost."

"I nearly did," I joked. "Navigating all the streets in this town requires talent."

Noah got out of the car and greeted me with a kiss on the cheek. It was polite, short and gave no hint of the familiarity between us. The whispered comment that came next wasn't so innocent. "I have it on good authority that you're very talented."

I took a step back and cleared my throat, trying to pull myself together and calm my thumping heart. Noah didn't seem to need any recovery time at all.

"Ready?" he asked, looking up at the house.

"Have you been here before?" I asked.

He glanced at me, his green eyes shining in the glow of the street light. "No," he replied. "I don't usually make house calls."

"Well this one will be a doozy," I warned. "An old witch lives here."

He huffed out a sharp laugh. "Edna's not a witch," he insisted. "She's just eccentric and odd. She's also forgetful, which is why I'm here."

As we fought our way past the weeds growing through the garden path, Noah explained why he was making an exception to his no-house-call rule.

"She's missed her last two appointments with me," he said, stopping dead at the edge of the steps.

His trepidation was warranted. The decking surrounding the house was a death-trap. Noah took my hand, leading me through the maze of holes and missing planks.

"I'm very worried about her dog," he continued.

"Why?" I asked.

Noah thumped loudly on the ancient front door. "Because she's a wiry old drunk."

I was sure he had his information wrong. I'd heard a million stories about crazy Edna in my time, but none of them involved booze. "Edna's an alcoholic?" I asked. "Are you sure?"

"No," he replied, wiggling his eyebrows. "Her bulldog is."

If I could've mustered words, it would've been too late to say them. The door swung open, and I came face-to-face with the stuff of nightmares.

"Hello, Mrs Wilson," Noah greeted. "I thought I'd stop by and visit Patty."

His cheery tone beggared belief. The old woman stared him down as if he'd just woken her from a hundred-year sleep – and the long white nightgown she wore led me to think that scenario wasn't entirely unrealistic.

She pushed her frizzy grey hair away from her

eyes. "She's sleeping," she replied. "Come back tomorrow."

Noah wedged his foot in the way of the closing door. "Mrs Wilson, have you met my friend, Lily?"

For the first time ever, I wanted to punch the city vet in the mouth.

"No," she replied, opening the door wide. "Introduce me to her."

I no longer thought she was just peculiar and crazy. Edna looked like a witch, and Edna spoke like a witch. Therefore, in my mind, she was a witch.

Noah didn't seem to share my opinion. He grabbed my hand and pulled me forward, thrusting me into her line of fire. Despite my terror, I managed to find my manners. "Nice to meet you, Mrs Wilson."

Her bony fingers wrapped around my hand, which was almost as disturbing as the look on her face. "Come inside and have a cup of tea," she urged, staring into my eyes. "You can share your gifts with me, and I'll return the favour."

I was too scared to ask what that meant, and

Noah was more interested in finding the boozed up bulldog. As we followed Edna down the long hallway, he paused at each doorway we passed to look for her.

"Patricia isn't accepting visitors," she told him, without looking back. "You'll have to see her another time."

"I'm just here to check on her." Noah's tone was still friendly, but there was an authoritative edge to it now. "She missed her last few appointments with me."

Ignoring him, Edna showed us into the kitchen, pointed at the shabby Formica dining suite and ordered us both to sit. "I'll make us some tea."

While we sat in silence, Edna fussed at the stove. I used the time to check out the room. Apart from the peeling paint and archaic whitegoods, it was just a regular kitchen – no cauldrons or lingering smell of boiling bones. The only thing out of place was the faint sound of snoring coming from somewhere behind us.

I turned around and saw nothing, but Noah wasn't fooled for a second. He traced the muffled sound to a laundry basket in the corner of the room. Without asking permission, he tossed a few layers of clothes aside and came face-to-face with Patricia the drunk French Bulldog.

"How much has she had to drink, Edna?" he asked crossly.

I wasn't sure how he could tell that she was sauced just by looking at her. She wasn't the prettiest dog I'd ever seen, which led me to think her drunk face was probably similar to her sober one.

"I've told you before," she replied. "She has a small tipple of brandy at night with her milk. The nights are cold, Noah."

He lifted the dazed dog out of the basket and tried to get her stand, catching her each time she stumbled. "I've told you before, Mrs Wilson, ethanol poisoning is very serious in dogs," he chided. "You have to trust me on this."

"I do," replied Edna, setting a pot of tea down on the table. "That's why I've cut her down to one drink before bed. It warms her guts up."

After checking Patty over, he tucked her back into the laundry basket, presumably to sleep it off.

"I have a better idea," he said, joining us at the table. "Lily is a pet couturier. She could design Patty a winter outfit to keep her warm. Then you could cut out the bedtime brandy."

Edna narrowed her eyes. "What sort of outfit?"

Still marvelling at the title of pet couturier, I struggled to answer her. "Anything you like."

The old lady picked up the teapot and poured all three cups of tea while she thought it through. "Patricia hails from the Highlands," she said finally. "She has Gaelic blood."

"She's Scottish?" asked Noah, trying not to smile.

"Perhaps not in this life," she conceded. "But originally."

I couldn't do anything about Patty's past lives, but I could try preserving her current one a little longer. I took my notepad out of my bag and went to work, sketching a very rough picture of a Scottish French Bulldog wearing a thick tartan coat. In keeping with her dubious Gaelic heritage, I added a tartan cap and threw in a pom-pom for good measure.

"How about something like this?" I asked, sliding the sketchpad across the table. "Do you think this would suit her?"

A huge smile swept Edna's face as she studied the picture in front of her. "A true Highland lass," she announced with reverence. "Patricia would be proud to wear this."

"Great," quipped Noah. "It'll be my gift to you, but you have to promise me something."

"Perhaps," said Edna staring at him through narrowed eyes. "Name your terms."

I already knew what they were, and realistically, she did too. Patty had to lay off the brandy and get sober. To me, it was a no-brainer, but Edna took time to deliberate. Finally, she dropped the sketchpad down on the table. "Fine," she agreed. "Measure her up, Lily. I want it tailored to perfection."

I learned something that night. When a dog is passed out drunk, taking its measurements is a breeze. While I sat at the table and wrote them down, Noah checked Patty over for the second time.

Edna's focus was solely on me. "This is your gift," she said, pointing at the notebook. "Making lovely things for man's best friends."

I nervously twirled my pencil between my fingers. "I guess so."

"You have to choose the fabric carefully," she continued. "Then put it all together."

I had no idea why she saw fit to give me instructions but found myself agreeing with her anyway.

"Then you cut off the useless frayed edges," she continued, lowering her tone as she leaned closer to me. "They contribute nothing to the finished product."

I shook my head. "No, they don't."

"You have no use for straggly edges, Lily." she explained. "Do you understand?"

I did understand, which could only mean one of two things: I was as cracked as she was, or Crazy Edna's psychic abilities weren't a crock after all.

"You're talking about my mum and my sister?" I asked, desperately seeking clarification.

She put a shaky hand on my cheek. "*Brutum*

fulmen," she whispered.

"What does that mean, Mrs Wilson?"

A normal person would've answered me, but Edna was far from normal. Instead, she stood up, carried the empty pot of tea to the sink and told us we had to leave.

***

In a perfect world, my first ever visit to crazy Edna's would've been an enlightening experience. All of the mystery shrouding the strange old woman would've been cleared up with logical explanations and an apology from me for being so judgmental. Evidently, the world wasn't perfect because I walked out of the house feeling more confused than ever.

Noah hung back at the door, laying down the law to Edna. "No more booze," he demanded. "And I want to see Patty next week."

"You can see her any time you want to," she replied. "Just make sure you bring her Highland coat with you."

Probably resigned to the fact that he wasn't

going to win, he called it quits. "Goodnight, Mrs Wilson."

I heard the door close and by the time I reached my car, Noah was right behind me. He looped his arm around my waist from behind and pulled me back against his chest. "Thank you," he whispered against the side of my neck.

"For what?"

"For being amazing," he replied. "And now I owe you dinner and a movie."

I twisted in his arms, needing to see his face when I broke the news that the whole world was closed for business. "It's eight o'clock on a Sunday night," I reminded him. "You'll have to settle for two-minute noodles and Netflix."

Smiling wryly, he slowly shook his head. "We can do better than that, surely," he said. "Perhaps not a movie, but dinner is doable."

I looked from left to right, emphasising the fact that the street was deserted. "Not here."

He leaned, murmuring his next words against my mouth. "Ten bucks says you're wrong."

"I don't have ten bucks." I felt his smile against

my lips. "I'm broke – totally down and out."

"I'm not an unreasonable man," he murmured. "I'll let you pay your debts in kind."

It was bet he was never going to win, but an impossible offer to refuse nonetheless. Without a moment of hesitation, I left my beaten up Audi parked on the street outside Edna's house and hitched a ride with the gorgeous but deluded city vet.

***

Once you drive beyond the outskirts of town, it's easy to make believe that you're a million miles away. I had no idea where we were heading, but it really didn't matter. The night was cool, the weather was fine, and the company was good.

Noah didn't seem to know where we were going either. Once he pulled onto the highway, he stayed there, and before long, we *were* a million miles from home. The conversation was light, and most of it centred around the strange evening we'd had so far.

"I'll try and get Patty's coat done tomorrow," I

offered. "The sooner the better, right?"

"Don't stress about it too much." Noah glanced across at me and smiled. "Patty has been on the turps for years. I think she's quite tolerant to her bedtime brandy so a few more days won't make much difference."

"Poor thing," I mumbled.

He reached, slipping his hand under the fall of my hair as he gently rubbed my neck. "I'm keeping a close eye on her, Lil," he assured me. "She'll be fine."

Moments like this reminded me why I was determined to keep our relationship secret. Noah Holt was righteous and good. He was also caring, brilliant and gorgeous inside and out. I was none of those things, which meant we were hardly a match made in heaven. As far as I was concerned, keeping quiet was doing him a favour. I was giving him an out, and sooner or later he'd be grateful for it.

***

Our journey into the great unknown came to an end at the most unlikely place imaginable — a petrol station in the middle of nowhere.

"Do we need fuel?" I asked.

"No," replied Noah, unclicking his seatbelt. "We're here for dinner."

At first, I thought he was joking, but then he got out of the car. I was in no hurry to move. As far as I was concerned, fast food from a servo made two-minute noodles seem like haute cuisine.

"I'm sensing reluctance, Lil," he said, opening my car door. "Or perhaps revulsion," he amended. "Have you ever eaten here?"

I shook my head. "I've never even stopped here for petrol."

There was no particular reason why. From what I could see, it was a perfectly fine establishment. The little independent station wasn't blanketed in fluorescent lights and huge windows like it's bigwig competitors. If not for the small forecourt and three bowsers at the front, the modest brick building could've passed as a house.

"The food is wonderful," Noah insisted, inching the car door wider. "As long as you have no aversion to chalkboard menus and bain-maries."

"Of course not," I lied, stepping out of the car.

"Glad to hear it." He took my hand in his. "Because I've got ten bucks riding on this dinner."

His smug tone was a little premature. When we reached the door, the closed sign caught my attention. "Shut happens," I read with a giggle. "That's cute."

Noah cupped his hands to the window and peered inside.

"We'll come back another time," I suggested, tugging on the back of his shirt.

"The lights are on."

"But nobody's home, Noah. Let's go."

"Somebody's always home." He flashed me a roguish grin. "There's a house at the back. Let's knock on the door." He was already walking away as he suggested it, and like a fool, I followed.

"Please tell me you know the people who live here." I skipped forward to stay close. "You're cute and all, but I'm not going to jail for you."

"If you get arrested, I'll use my ten bucks to bail you out." I could hear the smile in his voice. "I can't be fairer than that."

"And they say chivalry is dead," I muttered.

Without warning, he spun around and took me in his arms, dipping me back so swiftly that I closed my eyes, bracing for the crack of my head hitting the pavement.

It didn't happen, and when I looked up and saw his perfect face, I knew I was probably safer than I'd ever been in my whole life.

"I can be chivalrous," he murmured, kissing me to prove it.

I tightened my grip on his forearms. "Can we please go home?" I whispered.

He dropped his head, chasing my lips. "I am home."

As if on cue, a light came on. Noah straightened up, righting me in the process. The door behind him opened, and the sense of wrongdoing that had been plaguing me since I got out of the car disappeared in an instant.

The kindly looking lady in front of us didn't look miffed to see us. She was beaming, and only had eyes for the bloke standing next to me. "Noah George Sebastian Holt," she announced.

"Hi Mum," he greeted.

Discontented with the kiss on the cheek he gave her, she pulled him into a tight hug. "Where have you been, my boy?"

"Working." He motioned to me with a dip of his head. "And romancing this pretty girl in my spare time."

She stepped toward me, extending her hand. "You must be Lily."

I was astounded that she knew who I was, but I still managed to shake her hand. "It's nice to meet you, Mrs Holt."

She swatted the air between us. "Mrs Holt was my mother-in-law," she told me. "You can call me Trina."

That's where the formalities ended. With a wave of her hand, she ushered us inside and showed us through to the living room.

The inside of the Holt's house was as modest as the servo at the front. It was neat, homely and small. When Trina pointed at the couch, I followed her silent instruction and sat down. After shifting a few cushions and a stack of crossword puzzles, Noah sat beside me.

Ordinarily, meeting his mother for the first time would've been hugely daunting, but I wasn't feeling a skerrick of unease, mainly because Trina did all the talking.

It was like taking a crash course on Noah without having to study, and as chagrined as he might've been by her never-ending anecdotes, I was grateful for the insight.

Trina was very proud of her veterinarian son. The walls were lined with certificates and awards bearing his name, and she couldn't talk about Noah without smiling. "He was forever bringing home strays," she recalled. "Dogs, cats, you name it, he rescued it." She slapped her hands down on her knees and let out a hearty chuckle. "But he was always picky about the girls he brought home." She winked at me. "They had to be special to get his attention."

I'd been dating Noah for two short months. In that time, I'd been made to feel special a million times over, and if I could've verbalised that in a way that didn't sound creepy, I would've told her so. Instead, I smiled.

"Enough embarrassing stories, Mum," complained Noah. "We came here for hot chips and burgers."

Trina slapped her knees again – a gesture that was fast becoming her signature move. "The kitchen closed at eight."

"Don't make me look bad, Mum. Lily's already having doubts about me," he joked.

Letting out another hearty chuckle, Trina caved and rose to her feet. "I have my doubts about you too," she teased. "You don't visit your mother often enough."

***

While Trina indulged her son by going next door and reopening her kitchen, Noah showed me around. We ended up in the backyard, and that's when things got really interesting. As soon as I stepped outside, I got the eeriest feeling that we weren't alone – and when I heard rustling coming from the tall tree near the patio, I was sure of it.

I looked up, squinting into the mass of dark branches.

"What's the matter?" asked Noah.

"There's something in the tree," I whispered, moving closer to him. "I can hear it."

Far from alarmed, he grinned. "What do you think it is?"

"An elephant by the sound of it."

"Not quite." His arm slipped around me. "Peafowls. There are three of them."

"Peacocks?" I asked confused.

"Two peacocks," he clarified. "The blokes are peacocks; the ladies are peahens."

"And the babies are called peachicks?"

"No," he corrected. "Peababies."

I might've believed him if he hadn't ruined the lie by laughing.

"Wise arse," I chided, bumping his arm with my shoulder. "Why are they in the trees?"

Noah looked skyward. "They roost up there," he explained. "During the day, they hang out on the ground."

The darkness kept most of it hidden from view, but from what I could tell, Trina's backyard was the perfect habitat for them. The low-lying bracken and bushes extended all the way to the fence.

"How long have they been here?"

"Well, Cyril has been here for over twenty years," he replied. "I have a photo of him whooping it up at my tenth birthday party."

It may well have been the most magnificent story I'd ever heard, and it trumped Jasmine's scary birthday clown beyond measure.

I turned to Noah, trying not to look too awed. "Do you have any idea how interesting you are?"

"Some might consider it weird, Lil."

"No, I know weird, and believe me when I say you're not it." I stretched, linking my arms around his neck. "You're not a city vet either."

"No?" He sounded disappointed. "I quite like that tag."

"You grew up with a peacock called Cyril, and you lived at a roadhouse," I reminded him. "You're a bigger country hick than I am."

"I actually left here when I was eleven," he explained, slipping his hands into the back pockets of my jeans. "Six years of boarding school in

Hobart, and then university."

I let out an exaggerated sigh. "Fine," I grumbled. "Based on that information, we'll continue to mock and ridicule you on a daily basis – only now it'll be worse."

"Why?"

"Because you just admitted to being a private school boy."

"Excellent." His dark laugh travelled right through me. "Bring it on."

***

Before I even came close to finishing dinner, I had to concede that Noah had won the bet. After consuming a week's worth of calories, I could barely move, and it was worth every mouthful.

Trina didn't hang around to hear the praise I wanted to rain on her. After serving us the best junk food in existence, she bowed out in favour of an early night.

"I have to open up at four-thirty," she explained. "There's no rest for the wicked."

Noah stood up and hugged his mum. "Thank

you for dinner," he said, kissing her cheek.

"You're welcome," she said, patting his chest. "Don't wait until you're hungry before visiting your old mum again."

"I won't," he promised.

"And look after Lily," she called from the hallway. "Girls are much better than stray animals."

I leaned across the table to whisper to him. "I like your mum very much."

"I do too," he whispered back.

Meeting Noah's mother didn't inspire me to return the favour. If anything, I was more determined than ever to keep him away from the clan of misfits that I called family, and in a moment of weakness, I told him so.

"I'm sure I'd cope," he assured me.

I slowly shook my head, probably looking dire. "My mum is nothing like yours."

I'd given him enough information in the past few months for him to know that my family dynamics were less than ideal, and he'd seen the mayhem my sister was capable of firsthand.

"I'm not making any demands, Lil," he said quietly. "We have all the time in the world to get to know each other."

Keen to change the subject, I leaned back in my chair, feeling overly full and marginally sleepy. "I guess I owe you ten bucks."

"And I plan to collect on that debt," he replied, dropping his paper napkin on the table. "Just as soon as I recover from dinner."

8. LOVELY AND THRILLED

Charli

After spending a week scouting for locations, Lily finally decided that the doggie photoshoot would take place at my gallery. Considering it was empty, I thought it was a good choice, but Adam had a few reservations.

"What if the dogs make a mess?"

"We'll clean it up," I assured him. "No big deal."

I hooked my camera bag over my shoulder and called out to Bridget. "Get your shoes on, baby. We're leaving."

Adam took the heavy bag from me. "Promise you'll take it easy today?"

A few weeks ago, a request like that would never have crossed his lips, but things were different now. I was pregnant, and according to Adam, that made me fragile.

"You worry too much." I chastely kissed him. "But if you want to come down and check on me, I'll be there for most of the day."

Chances were, I was going to need him there at some point anyway. Gabrielle's canvas backdrops had been hung, and the props were in place, but we'd done it ourselves so none of it was likely to hold for long.

Bridget rocketed down the hallway, waving a pink sneaker in each hand. "I'm ready now," she squealed. "We should get out of here."

The urgency was all in her little mind, but I appreciated the enthusiasm, and so did Lily. When we met her at the gallery fifteen minutes later, Bridget rushed at her from the door.

"It's your happy, happy day today, Lil!" Her shrill little voice echoed through the entire building. "The dog photo day!"

Lily scooped her up and hugged her. "How exciting," she replied, lowering her to her feet.

I wasn't sure that excitement was the right

sentiment, but I couldn't deny that I was eager to make the day a success. Lily had a lot riding on it, and we'd worked tirelessly to pull it together.

Gabrielle had worked her Parisienne butt off too, namely transforming the white canvas drop sheets into brilliant pieces of art. The grungy, urban paint job was graffiti-like in style, and it meshed with the wooden floor and whitewashed walls of the gallery seamlessly.

"Like a New York loft apartment," she told us. "Don't you think?"

I agreed, but Lily didn't answer the question. Instead, she thanked her – for the millionth time that week.

Gabrielle liked to feel appreciated as much as anyone else, but this was overkill and it was starting to make her twitchy. She turned to Lily, putting both hands on her shoulders. "I have enjoyed this project immensely," she said, giving her a shake. "And you have been a revelation."

Lily frowned, looking worried. "Why?"

Gabrielle dropped her hands to her sides and let out a long sigh. "For years, I loathed sushi," she began. "It's raw, unrefined and unappealing."

Conversations with the Parisienne usually take some deciphering, but not even I knew what she was talking about. "You've lost us, Gabs."

She continued as if I hadn't spoken, focusing only on Lily. "One day Alex made me try it."

"And?" Lily's voice was tiny. "What happened?"

"I loved it," she replied, flashing her beauty queen grin. "You are like sushi, Lily Tate. After years of avoiding you, I tried you, and you're wonderful."

The strange compliment hit Lily hard. Her blue eyes welled with tears. "Thank you," she choked.

I cocked my head, whispering from the corner of my mouth. "Lil, you realise she just compared you to raw fish, right?"

"Shut up," she mumbled, bumping me with her shoulder. "I like sushi."

***

Gabrielle's vision stretched far beyond the set design. She'd also taken care of costuming, supplying one of her own gowns for Lily to wear during the shoot. The emerald green, floor-length silk number was elegant and glamourous – and in complete contrast to her grungy inner-city set.

It was as left-of-centre as she was, but despite my reservations, it worked. The only person who wasn't on board was Lily. After getting dressed, she shuffled out of the back room with a handful of dress in each hand, trying her best to keep it from dragging on the floor.

"You look lovely," praised Bridget, wildly clapping her hands. "Like a green frog."

"Thanks, Bridge," she mumbled.

Gabrielle agreed. "Almost a perfect fit," she said, fussing with the neckline.

Lily smoothed the front of the dress with both hands. "I'm not sure about this. I feel a bit overdressed."

Reverting to her old schoolmarm ways, Gabi slapped her hands away. "Nonsense," she snapped. "You look perfect."

On the off chance that she was about to bust out another sushi lecture, I decided to escape while I could. "Let's go, Bridge," I said, reaching for her hand. "You can help me set the camera up."

Bridget abandoned her pile of girls on the floor and scrambled to her feet. "I will take some photos too." She spoke as if it was a given. "I just love dog pictures."

***

Everything was good to go.

The set was complete, Lily's stage fright was under control, and Gabi had slowed her bossy roll. After making a few last minute changes to her arty backdrop, she retired the cans of spray-paint and cleaned the paint off her hands. "My work here is done," she announced, wringing her hands on a rag.

"You're leaving?" asked Lily incredulously.

"She has to," I said, answering for her. "She likes Alex too much to stay."

My father's allergy to dogs was severe. If Gabi arrived home caked in dog hair, he'd be in an antihistamine haze for days.

"I want to go home too," Bridget chimed in. "I've had enough now."

Somewhere along the line, Bridget's enthusiasm had given way to boredom. She'd been well behaved until that point, but cracks were beginning to show. As I wrenched a can of spray-paint from my daughter's hand, I asked Gabi if she could hitch a ride with her.

"Of course." Gabrielle slung her big tote bag over her shoulder. "Jack will be thrilled to see her."

"Yes he will," agreed Bridget, grabbing Gabi's hand. "Lovely and thrilled."

***

Once Gabi and Bridget left, I was more than ready to get the show on the road, but one important element was missing. "What time are the pooches arriving?" I asked, checking the time on my watch.

"Any minute now," replied Lily. "Although I'm expecting Nancy to be late."

"Why?"

She grimaced, looking pained. "Because Jasmine is bringing her."

I groaned, unable to hide my frustration. "That means she's going to see what we're doing here."

And letting her in on that secret meant our theatrics in the hardware store the week before had been a complete waste of effort.

"Why would you tell her, Lil?" I growled.

"I didn't have a choice," she defended. "It's the only way she'd let me have Nancy for the day."

I wanted to scream at her and demand that she grow a backbone, but yelling would've done more harm than good. Jasmine had been getting the better of her for years, and until Lily could figure out how to break the sparkly cycle of abuse, it was going to continue.

I swallowed hard, trying to quell the annoyance. "How many dogs are coming?" I asked calmly.

"Just three. Nancy is the small model, and I'm borrowing a Cocker Spaniel and a Lab from Noah," she explained. "That way, we have a small, medium and large."

I no longer gave a hoot about the doggie headcount. I had no clue who Noah was, and I wanted to know more.

Unfortunately, the explanation she gave wasn't that interesting. Noah Holt was the new vet in town, and because Nancy was a million years old and in poor health, Lily dealt with him often.

"He's really good with animals," she said.

I couldn't help laughing. "That's a good quality in a vet, I guess."

It was a pointless but funny conversation that was cut short when the front door opened. Neither of us batted an eye when Jasmine traipsed in with Nancy in tow, but when we saw who was with her, the whole game changed.

I hadn't seen Lisa Reynolds since high school, but there was no mistaking it was her. From what I could see, she hadn't changed much. She was tall, lean and probably still mean.

"Look who I found," crowed Jasmine, pointing at Lisa as if we needed a hint.

Refusing to react, Lily and I stood side-by-side, watching as they slowly sauntered towards us. My whole high school career played out in my head in the time it took them to cross the gallery floor, and most of it was ugly.

Obviously Lily was on the same track. "This is very bad, Charli," she whispered from the corner of her mouth.

The threat of a Beautifuls reunion was of no concern to me, but she was right to be worried. I'd left that brand of terror behind a long time ago, but Lily was a different story. She was as vulnerable now as she'd always been, and there was nothing I could do to save her.

Probably disappointed by the cool reception, Jasmine tried harder. "It's been eight years," she hissed. "Show a bit of love."

Lisa let out a condescending cackle. "It's fine," she said. "They're probably just shocked to see me."

"Not shocked," Lily clarified. "Confused, maybe." She roughly snatched Nancy's lead from her sister's grasp. "I was under the impression that Jasmine was happy when you left town. She said she hated you."

Jasmine gasped. "I never said that!"

I would've bet money that she did, and Lisa didn't look too shocked by the claim either. "Who cares?" Her shoulders lifted. "We were kids. A lot has changed since then."

And in true Lisa style, she felt compelled to spend the next few minutes telling us all about it. "I've been working in Sydney. I'm an engineer, you know." Perhaps mindful that Jasmine was the only who seemed interested, she focused on her. "A very high powered job – plenty of responsibility, great money."

"What are you doing back here then?" Lily snapped.

I dropped my head, directing my inappropriate giggle at the floor. I had no idea where Lily's sudden rush of douche-like behaviour had come from, but I wanted to pat her on the back and congratulate her for it.

"The Cove is my home," said Lisa, glowering at her. "I belong here as much as you do."

"Of course you do." Jasmine hooked her arm though hers. "And we're thrilled to have to you back, right Lily?"

"If you say so."

Thanks to Lily's refusal to back down, Jasmine's efforts when it came to reuniting her bitchy crew were failing, but Lisa wasn't the least bit daunted by the hostility. Instead, she moved on to me. "And what about you, Charli?" she asked, looking me up and down. "What have you been up to?"

Jasmine would've brought her up to speed long before that moment so answering her in any detail would've been a waste of breath. "Not much," I replied. "A bit of this, a bit of that."

"Still taking photos, I see." She wandered over to my tripod, prowling around it like a lion before turning her attention to Gabrielle's arty backdrop. "This is cute."

"What's it supposed to be?" asked Jasmine. "A modelling shoot?"

When Jasmine turned to her sister and slowly looked her up and down, Lily's resolve began to slip before my very eyes. That's when my mouth got the better of me.

"It is, actually," I embellished. "A fashion buyer from New York is extremely interested in Lily's pet designs. They've asked for some professional shots."

Lisa's kohl rimmed eyes narrowed with suspicion. "Really?" she drawled.

Lily's ensuing cough sounded a lot like terror, but I held firm. "Yes," I replied. "Fashion week is coming up soon."

September was eight months away, but it was my lie and I was running with it. "Lily's designs may well be gracing the catwalk this year."

Jasmine's eyes looked close to bugging out of her head, but Lisa barely reacted. "We should leave you alone to get on with it then." Her smile was tight. "Making Lily and a bunch of dogs look worthy of fashion week will probably take time."

"Yeah," agreed Jasmine, pulling a face. "Your makeup is terrible, Lil."

A good friend of Lily's would've bitten back with a snarky comeback while pushing them both out the door, but I had no skill when it came to being a good friend.

I was a good liar, though.

"They're not interested in the models," I said. "It's her designs that are worth the big bucks."

Jasmine's eyes drifted to the mobile clothes rack that was overflowing with doggie clothes. "How big?"

Mercifully, I didn't have to answer. The front door swung open again, and everyone turned to see why.

"Noah," breathed Lily, handing me Nancy's lead. Clearly no longer concerned about the hem of her dress dragging on the floor, she hurriedly rushed to greet him.

Her enthusiasm was understandable. Noah the vet was not the dorky Doctor Dolittle I was expecting, and I wasn't the only one who took a second glance.

Lisa leaned over and whispered to Jasmine, "who is that? He's cute."

He was not cute. A man who can make the combination of Blundstone boots and a neat dress shirt look good is never merely cute. Noah Holt was handsome and debonair – and a million miles out of the Beautifuls' league.

"Come," hissed Jasmine, grabbing Lisa's sleeve. "I'll introduce you to him."

I had zero interest in watching the try-hards make their play, but it was impossible not to listen.

"Noah, this is Lisa," pitched Jasmine. "She's my

oldest and dearest friend."

It wasn't exactly a ringing endorsement. Being besties with Jasmine was hardly a coup, and in my opinion, Lisa was no prize either.

"Nice to meet you," he politely replied.

Noah didn't seem remotely interested in anything Jasmine had to say. He was more focused on the two dogs roughhousing at his feet. Lily stepped forward and took control of the smaller dog, and the smile he gave as he handed her the leash was warmer than anything he'd shown her bolshie sister.

Still, Jasmine pressed on. "She just arrived back in the Cove after a long stint on the mainland," she explained.

"I'm an engineer," interjected Lisa, sounding too stupid for words.

"Right," said Noah. "Welcome home then, I guess."

"It's good to be here." Lisa flicked her blonde hair off her shoulder. "I'm single and ready to mingle."

I heard someone groan, and after studying their

faces, I decided it must've been Lily. She looked mortified.

Putting an end to the nonsense wasn't going to be easy, but I tried. "Can we hurry this along, please?" I called.

"Yes, please," replied Noah, sounding far too grateful. "I've got to get back to work." He handed the other leash to Lily. "Just call me when you're finished and I'll pick them up," he offered.

Lily grabbed his arm. "Before you go, come and meet Charli." She motioned toward me with a stiff nod. "She'd love to say hi."

"Enough introductions, Lil," Jasmine chided. "He doesn't need to meet the whole town."

Knocking Lily down with child-like rebukes was something Jasmine did often. It was designed to make her feel stupid, but this time it fell short.

"One more introduction can't hurt," said Noah. "I've almost forgotten the first one."

Lisa Reynolds must've had a cast iron soul. His cutting comment bounced right off her. "Don't worry about it," she said, granting him a sordid smile. "I'm sure there will be plenty of time to get to know each other."

"Another day," said Jasmine, pulling her trampy mate toward the door.

I didn't watch them leave, but I knew they had. The sound of the front door slamming echoed through the entire building.

We were finally free to get on with our day, but Lily needed a minute to gather herself. Without saying a word, she handed the leashes back to Noah and took off to the makeshift dressing area in the back room.

Probably having no clue what else to do, Noah slowly walked his dogs over to me. "I'm guessing you're Charli?"

His rigid expression made me smile. "Relax, Noah," I urged. "I'm not single, and I'm not going to force you to mingle."

He huffed out a sharp laugh. "Thank God for that."

My eyes drifted down to the dogs. "So, do these blokes have names?"

"The little one is Honey, and her fat friend's name is Hank," he replied.

"Well, Hank," the chunky old Lab's ears went back as I said his name, "I'm not sure how you're going to handle today. Didn't anyone ever tell you that the camera adds ten pounds?"

"Go easy on him," teased Noah. "He has confidence issues."

He wasn't the only one. Lily rushed back into the room waving a small toiletry bag at me. "We need to redo my makeup," she said in a trembly voice. "Jasmine was right. I look like rubbish."

"No one looks like rubbish when they're wearing a Valentino gown," I retorted. "Suck it up. You look fine."

"More than fine," corrected Noah. "I think you look beautiful, Lil."

I wasn't sure what was driving her at that point, but it wasn't common sense. If she'd been thinking straight at all, she would've cottoned on that the handsome vet was flirting with her – which is far more progress than her ex-teammates had made.

When she thrust the makeup bag at me, I stumbled back, almost stepping on Nancy in the process. "Just try and fix it up," she urged. "Please, Charli."

"I'm not qualified to use eyeliner, Lil," I protested. "Even on myself."

Noah let out a dark chuckle. "I think I'll leave you ladies to it." He handed control of Hank and Honey to Lily. "Call me when you're done, okay?"

"I will," she promised. "And thanks for letting me borrow the dogs."

"Any time," he replied already walking away.

9. All BARK AND NO BITE

Lily

Those who need to feel superior are usually prepared to pull out all stops to make sure it happens. I didn't know if Lisa's return to town was tactical or coincidental, but it reinforced Jasmine's superiority complex no end.

Her half-arsed attempts at winning me back were over. As long as she had her long lost number-two back by her side, she had no use for me, but that didn't mean I'd be left in peace. I'd spent years playing the role of chew toy, and from what I could tell, nothing had changed.

It didn't take a genius to work out that life was going to get infinitely trickier. Spending a few years on the mainland hadn't changed Lisa Reynolds one bit. She was still bitchy, spiteful and mean – and no matter how hard I tried not to be, I was still scared of her.

I wasn't the only one who'd reverted to the mindset of a vulnerable fifteen-year-old girl. Whether she'd cop to it or not, they'd gotten the better of Charli too, and her stupid fashion week lie proved it.

"Why would you say that?" I spat the frantic question at her. "You know they're not just going to forget about it."

Charli continued fussing with her camera, probably in a bid to avoid eye contact. "I'm sorry," she muttered contritely. "It just came out of nowhere."

It was an easy answer, but not the truth. She'd felt as intimated as I had, and had said something dumb because of it.

"You've just made the situation worse," I growled.

"There is no situation," she replied. "They're not focused on tormenting us. Lisa has her eye on Noah. He'll be the one fending off the sparkly blows from now on."

It was an appalling prospect, but I didn't fess up and tell her why. It was a betrayal that didn't sit well with me. Charli had gone up and above for me lately – for no other reason than friendship – and I wasn't giving her much in return.

"Let's just get this done," I muttered, smoothing down the front of my dress. "We'll deal with the rest later."

***

Whoever coined the phrase that one should never work with children or animals was speaking the absolute truth.

Nancy was far too old and too set in her ways to deal with the spritely combination of Honey and Hank. After just a few snaps of the camera, she leapt off my lap and hid behind the canvas backdrop.

Honey was well behaved, but Hank was slow and dopey. Every time he wagged his tail, he knocked something over. Charli had to make a grab for the tripod more than once, and it wasn't long before she called it quits.

"We were idiots to think we could do this by ourselves," she said, reaching for her phone. "We need help."

"Who are you calling?" I asked, grabbing Hank's collar as he passed.

"Adam," she replied. "He's a New Yorker. That automatically qualifies him to deal with stroppy fashion models."

From what I could tell, there wasn't much that Adam wouldn't do for Charli. He arrived within the hour, rolled up his sleeves and tried his hand at playing costume manager for the afternoon.

I'm sure he didn't enjoy it, and none of the dogs made it easy for him, but he didn't complain. The of Hero of the Day title was his, but when it was all over, he went the extra mile and helped us tidy up.

While Charli was occupied packing away her camera equipment, I stole a quick moment to thank him.

"No problem," he replied flashing me a dimpled smile. "It was almost fun."

"Hopefully we got some good shots." I looked

at the half dismantled set. "Everyone has gone to so much trouble."

It was a notion that almost bothered me. I'd been shown more grace and goodwill in the past few weeks than ever before, and I was grateful, but there was a cynical part of my soul that kept waiting for the other shoe to drop.

"That's what friends do, Lily," he replied.

Adam Décarie wasn't remotely close to being a friend of mine. He was ten times more intimidating than Lisa could ever hope to be, but not because he was evil.

By all accounts, he was kind, generous and sweet. But Adam also had an air of elitism that made him hard to talk to, and impossible to relate to.

Pushing awkwardness aside, I tried to keep the conversation alive. "Adam, can I ask you something?"

He shrugged. "Sure."

"You speak French, right?"

The dumb question made him laugh. "A little."

When the floor failed to open up and swallow

me, I cleared my throat and pressed on. "I was hoping you could translate something for me."

I didn't want to explain the ins and outs of my visit to Edna's, so I got straight down to business and hit him with the two words that had been playing on my mind all week. My pronunciation sucked, but he got the gist.

"*Brutum fulmen*," he corrected with a smile. "And it's not French, it's Latin."

"You speak Latin too?" I asked incredulously.

He pinched his thumb and forefinger together. "A little."

His sheepish expression led me to think he was seriously downplaying his skills, but I let it go. "What does it mean?"

"Well, it quite literally means a harmless thunderbolt."

I frowned, none the wiser. "Okay," I replied, dejected. "Thanks."

Adam folded his arms and leaned in closer. "Do you want the deeper meaning, Lil?"

"Yes, please," I mumbled, nodding my head. "I think it might be important."

He straightened up, smiling brightly. "A harmless bolt of thunder is useless – loud enough to scare you, but powerless to hurt you," he explained. "All bark and no bite."

Confusion suddenly gave way to wonderment. Edna's scary ramble had been about Jasmine – Lisa too if her witchy powers extended that far.

"Does it make sense?" he asked.

In a move that neither of us would ever have predicted, I lurched forward and hugged him tightly. "More than you'll ever know," I replied.

10. SUSHI LEVEL BEAUTIFUL

Charli

When I was a conniving teenager, telling lies to get myself out of tight spots was commonplace. It rarely worked, which probably explains why I gave it up. It was a trait that I was glad to be rid of, but the events of that day proved that I was only ever one wicked deed away from being the ratbag girl I used to be.

Making up stories about bogus fashion buyers had set Lily up for certain failure. The Beautifuls were never going to let it go and were likely to mock her until the end of time because of it. The stress of that realisation had nearly caused Lily to melt down, and I was entirely responsible.

It was still playing on my mind hours after I arrived home, and confessing my sins to Adam didn't make me feel any less wretched. "It was a stupid, thoughtless thing to do," I told him. "Lily won't handle the fallout."

"Charlotte, they're grown women," he reminded me. "There shouldn't be any fallout."

Adam didn't recognise the problem at hand because he'd never understood the complicated hierarchy to begin with. I wasn't interested in explaining it to him. I was too busy trying to figure out a solution. "I'm going to upload the pictures to the website," I mumbled. "Lily's waiting on them."

When I picked up my laptop bag, he took it from me. "I'm glad that you're friends with her, Charli." He didn't sound the least bit believable. "But I don't want you to take Lily's drama on board."

I wrestled the computer away from him. "My big mouth caused her drama today, Adam."

He followed me to the dining room. "It can't be the same as it was before," he warned. "If being friends means dealing with the same juvenile crap that you put up with ten years ago, there's no point to it."

I thumped the computer down on the table

much harder than I should've. "I'm not putting up with anything," I snapped. "I'm just going to try and right a wrong."

"And then?"

I studied his concerned face, pondering his question. "And then I'll leave it alone."

He reached, placing his hand on my stomach. "We have better things to be concerned about, Charli."

I completely agreed, but saying it out loud would've felt like giving in so I said nothing. The new friendship that was blossoming between Lily and me was easy, uncomplicated and fresh. If the resurgence of the Beautifuls changed that, I had to be prepared to call it quits. I was finally in a good place, and if Lily could find her way clear of Jasmine and Lisa, she could be too.

In the time it took my computer to fire up, I hatched a quick plan. Putting an end to the fashion week debacle would level Lily's playing field. From there, she could either run with the ball or lay down and let her sister trample her.

The choice was hers, and hers alone.

***

I had taken a phenomenal amount of photos that day, and getting them uploaded to the Pawesome Designs website took forever. My favourites were the shots of Lily; dolled up in the Valentino gown with a regal-looking Nancy on her lap.

I emailed them to her straight way, keen to show her that my Photoshopping skills weren't required. I then followed up with a quick text reiterating the fact that every bit of stress we'd endured that day was worth it.

– **Sushi level beautiful.**

Her reply was simple but Lily to a T; a long run of happy face emojis that ended with a love heart.

***

After spending the afternoon squeezing dogs into tuxedos, ball gowns and hoodies, Adam took a long shower before heading out to pick Bridget up. When he called an hour later to let me know they were on their way home, I was still uploading photos.

Knowing I only had minutes before Cyclone

Bridget hit, I made an early morning phone call to Manhattan.

Bente answered straight away, giving me hope that I hadn't woken her. "I'm on my way to work," she told me. "And it's freaking freezing this morning."

"I'll make it quick," I promised. "I have a favour to ask."

It was a relief to know she was pressed for time. Bente was a stickler for details, but being in a hurry meant she had no time to hear them.

"My friend has just started a new business. She's a dog couturier."

"A doggie designer?" I could hear the smile in her voice. "That's a new one."

"She's really talented," I pitched. "The problem is that she's having trouble getting her brand out there. I was hoping you could run a story about her in the Tribune."

It was the longest of longshots, but I figured anything was worth a try. An article in the Manhattan Tribune and a glowing endorsement from my influential mother-in-law could potentially give Pawesome Designs a huge kick start.

But Bente wasn't exactly sold. All I could hear was the sound of background traffic, which meant she'd either dropped her phone or was too outraged to speak.

"Say something," I urged.

"I'm not sure, Charli," she said finally. "I've only been there a few months. I don't get a say when it comes to the stories they run."

"Please, just try," I begged.

Her trademark husky laugh filtered through the phone. "No pressure, right?"

"None," I assured her. "You live with Ryan. You deal with enough pressure."

Her laugh got louder. "I have to go," she replied. "Leave it with me and I'll get back to you."

I ended the call feeling marginally optimistic that Bente would come through for me, but I wasn't prepared to jump the gun and let Lily in on the plan. Until her name was in print, it was little more than a hopeful case of nothing ventured, nothing gained.

11. FALLING SHORT

Lily

The downward slide can be unceremoniously fast. Despite the fact that my website now looked as professional as any top level retailer, the sales were abysmal. After a month, I'd sold three outfits, and that included Patty's highlander coat.

To make matters worse, a costly but necessary repair to my wreck of an Audi had chewed through the last of my savings. Professionally, I was in absolute dire straits, and holding my personal life together was no picnic either.

Charli's prediction that Lisa would set her sights on Noah came to fruition after less than a week, and it was a relentless campaign that extended as far as buying a kitten just so she'd have reason to see him.

As expected, the city vet wasn't coping well with the unwanted attention. At first, he was nice to her, and when that didn't work he resorted to being curt and short, but nothing worked. Lisa Reynolds was abnormally resilient – and all she had to show for her efforts was a hypochondriac kitten and mounting vet bills.

In Noah's mind, I was the key to putting an end to the nonsense. All I had to do was lay claim and let her know that he was off limits. "It'll kill two birds with one stone," he reasoned. "Lisa will leave me alone, and her cat will make a miraculous recovery."

He made a joke of it, but there was nothing remotely funny about the situation. For three months I'd been trying to convince myself that I was worthy of him. Given the latest set of circumstances, I was more certain than ever that I wasn't. And if I didn't believe it, no one else was going to buy it either.

"I can't, Noah," I weakly mumbled. "The less I have to deal with Lisa and Jasmine at the moment, the better."

I made it sound like an inconvenience that I didn't have time for, which pissed him off. I could see the tension in his jaw, but he remained calm. We were in his office, and with a crowd of furry patients waiting in the next room, the tough conversation could go no further.

He stabbed a syringe into a vial of clear liquid and drew back the plunger. "I left high school a decade ago, Lil," he told me. "I have no interest in revisiting that petty drama either."

"I'm sorry." My voice was pathetically weak. "Sooner or later they'll move on and leave you alone."

"It'd be sooner if you just speak up." He carefully delivered the shot to the scruff of Nancy's neck. "I was under the impression we have something special going on."

"We do," I insisted.

"So why does it feel so one sided?" he asked, handing Nancy a chewy treat.

He had every right to question it. All he was asking me to do was set the record straight, and by not speaking up, I was giving him the impression that our romance was casual and disposable.

"I'm doing the best I can, Noah."

Frustratingly, the despair I was feeling was absent from my tone. I sounded arrogant and uncaring, and the glint of hurt in his eyes showed the damage it had caused.

He clipped Nancy's leash on her collar. "Your best is falling short, Lily," he replied. "Maybe you should work on that."

The level of hurt in my heart was rising to my brain. I couldn't think straight. Was he dumping me? I didn't know, and it was excruciating.

I scooped Nancy off the bench and held her close. "I need to work on a lot of things." I frantically blinked, trying to keep the tears from spilling over. "Grab a number and get in line."

***

Despite a strong start, my friendship with Charli had cooled over the past few weeks. We had compatibility issues. While my life was falling to pieces, her world was overflowing with sunshine and roses. The Décaries' were busier than ever.

Bridget had just started school and the news that a new baby was on the way was all over town.

I had no interest in playing the role of wet blanket, but after my confusing exchange with Noah, I was desperate to share my woes with Charli.

After delivering Nancy to Jasmine's I called in on the way home.

Adam was loading a set of golf clubs into the back of his ute. I got out of the car and wandered toward him, but my eyes were firmly on Bridget, who was standing on the lawn waving a putter around like a sword.

"I see you got the Audi back on the road," he noted. "What was the problem with it?"

"Something to do with the transmission," I vaguely replied. "All I know is that it cost me a bomb to fix it."

"Ouch." He smiled then, which was unusual for Adam. He usually grimaced when talking about the once pristine car he used to own.

"I'll get over it." I shrugged. "What are you up to?"

Bridget rushed over, coming to a grinding halt by her dad's side. "We're going to play golf!" she excitedly squealed.

"No school today?"

"No, Lily." She giggled as if it was a stupid question. "No school for girls on Friday. Today is Friday."

"So it is," I replied, grinning at her. "Aren't you too small for golf?"

"No, I'm lovely at it," she boasted. "I can kick that ball's big butt."

She tried to follow up with a swing of her club, but Adam snatched it from her. The apology he gave was directed at me, but the harsh frown was reserved solely for his errant daughter.

I vaguely pointed in the direction of the house. "I just stopped by to see Charli," I explained. "Is she in?"

"Yeah," he replied. "Golf isn't her thing."

"Golf is my thing," said Bridget, tugging on his shirt. "Please, Daddy. Let's go now."

"Yes," I agreed, grateful for the escape. "Don't let me hold you up."

A freak hurricane wouldn't have held them up. Adam bundled Bridget and her smart mouth into the car, and was backing out of the driveway before I even made it to the house.

I stepped up onto the porch and quietly knocked. Charli appeared a few seconds later, but spoke to me through the screen door. I couldn't blame her for the cool reception. I'd been rudely avoiding her for days.

"I've left you a hundred messages lately," she said. "You never return my calls. What's the deal, Lil?"

"I'm sorry," I said sincerely. "I've had a lot on my plate, but if you're still up for it, I could really use a friend right now."

The younger, hot-headed version of Charli probably would've slammed the door in my face, but the new and improved Charli was much more forgiving. She opened the door, invited me inside and offered to make me tea.

The conversation took a while to get going, mainly because I had no idea where to start but by our third cup, there was no shutting me up. I started with the epic failure of Pawesome Designs.

Clearly, it blindsided her. "I had no idea things were that bad." Her brown eyes were wide, and her frown was strong. "Every time I ask you about it, you tell me it's going well."

I stared down at my mug of tea, unable to look at her. "I lied. I've sold nothing."

Charli reached across the table and put her hand on mine. "I'm so sorry, Lily," she said. "I know how hard you worked on it."

She'd given it her all too, perhaps that's why she looked so crushed.

"I'm out of money so it's pretty much the end of the line. Fixing my car chewed through the last of my savings." I spoke as if it was no big deal, but inside I was dying. "I'm going to have to admit defeat and get a real job."

She straightened up in her seat. "Can't you hold out a little bit longer?"

When I asked why her explanation came at warp speed. In the coolest marketing ploy ever, she'd approached her journalist sister-in-law about running an article in the New York newspaper she worked for.

"Not only would it be great for business, but it would shut your bitch sister and her sidekick down in a second."

Weeks had passed since Charli's fashion week blunder, but I was still paying the price. Lisa and Jasmine never missed the opportunity to rib me about it, and the further Pawesome Designs slipped into the red, the harder it was to keep the lie going.

"I keep telling them a deal is in the works." It was an admission that made me cringe. "I'm going to have to come clean eventually – probably while I'm begging Jasmine for my job back."

Charli let out a pained groan. "Just hold out a bit longer, Lil," she desperately urged. "I'll talk to Bente again. If that article goes ahead, business will boom. You won't have to come clean about anything."

I slowly shook my head. "I'm broke, Charli. It's done."

"I can lend you some money."

My reply got caught in a humourless laugh. "I'm not taking money from you. I'm not a charity case."

Her posture crumpled as her shoulders dropped. "Of course not," she replied. "I didn't mean to imply otherwise."

We were quiet for a while, but I was okay with that. Endings are usually subdued.

I used the time to work out how to broach Noah – the next subject of doom. But Charli's mind was still on figuring out how to drag me back from financial ruin.

"What about a bank loan?" she blurted. "That might buy you some breathing space."

Until then, I'd never even considered it, and I wasn't too arrogant to admit that I had no clue how to go about applying for one.

Charli shrugged. "I don't know either, but we could go down to the bank and find out."

Never one to hold back, she rose to her feet and grabbed her car keys, and before I could really think things through, we were walking out the door.

12. EMPIRE OF DIRT

Charli

The Pipers Cove branch of the Bank of Hobart was located on the main street. Unlike the original bank building that Adam renovated, it was modern, generic and charmless.

While Lily approached the teller, I hung back by the plastic pot plants near the door, trying hard not to look like I was casing the joint. After a minute of hushed chatter, the woman directed Lily to a row of chairs near the front windows.

"She wants me to talk to a loan officer."

Her inconvenienced tone made me laugh.

"Did you think they were just going to hand over a wad of cash, Lil?"

She let out a quiet chuckle of her own and sat down. "I was hoping so."

The beauty of living in a small town is that you're never kept waiting long. We'd only been seated for a few minutes when one of the nearby office doors opened.

I didn't know the man who walked out to greet us, but Lily seemed to, and judging by her ashen face, she wasn't pleased to see him. "Don't leave my side," she whispered from the corner of my mouth. "Not even for a second."

"I'm not going anywhere," I assured her.

As soon as she was within reach, he extended his hand to Lily. "Garret Carmichael."

She reluctantly met his handshake but pulled away quickly. "Lily Tate."

I didn't bother introducing myself. I was merely there for moral support, and from what I could tell, she needed it. I just wasn't sure why.

Garret showed us through to his office; another generic room with flat pack furniture and uncomfortable chairs. He sat down opposite us and pushed a stack of brochures toward Lily. "Why don't you tell me a bit about yourself."

I wasn't exactly well versed on bank protocol,

but his question seemed better suited to a Friday night at the pub rather than a loan interview.

Lily looked down at the brochures, nervously thumbing through them as she tried her best to explain her Pawesome Designs venture. "I'm just looking at a small loan to –"

Garret cut her off with a click of his fingers that made us both jump. "I know where I know you from." He leaned back in his chair and flicked his tie. "The Castle Flats Footy Club, right?"

Lily emphatically shook her head. "No, I don't think so."

Not even I bought her weak answer, and Garret continued as if she hadn't spoken at all.

"You were one of the A-girls." He turned his attention to me. "We never even came close to winning a premiership, but the A-girls made up for any skills we were lacking." He followed up with a wink that made my stomach lurch.

Even with the limited information he'd given me, I knew Garett was revisiting a place Lily didn't want to go. Her face was as white as a sheet and her hands were trembling.

"Can we just get back to the business at hand, please?" I asked.

"Sure, sure," he replied, flashing Lily a sordid grin. "The floor is yours – just like old times, eh?"

I would've stood up and stormed out at that point, but Lily stayed put. She cleared her throat and determinedly continued her pitch as if she had something to prove.

The douche wasn't even listening. "Do you still go to the club, Lily?" He didn't pause long enough to hear her answer. "I still live in Sorell, but I haven't been in years." He patted his paunch and flicked his tie again. "Too old and fat now for those kinds of shenanigans, eh?"

Garret Carmichael could only have been a few years older than us, and he wasn't particularly fat. He was, however, an arsehole.

Finally at the end of her rope, Lily shoved the brochures across the desk. "I think we're done."

"Wait," he said desperately. "Before you go, take my card." He opened his desk drawer and slid a business card across the desk. "It's got my mobile number on the back… just in case you feel like catching up over a drink or something."

Lily turned to me and hissed out a desperate question. "Can we go?"

"Not yet," I replied, staring at Captain Dickhead. "I want to close my accounts," I announced. "I'm extremely dissatisfied with the service at this bank." Garett had the nerve to look insulted, and he didn't exactly rush to accommodate my request. "Can you do it from here or do I need to speak to a teller?" I asked, pushing him along.

He tilted the screen of his computer, angling it away from us. "As long as you've got your account details, I can do it from here," he said flatly. "Clients come and go all the time. No big deal."

"You won't miss my business then," I replied, slapping my ATM card down on the desk.

Garett meticulously keyed in my account number before pausing to study the details on the screen. Then it was our turn to watch the colour drain from *his* face. I couldn't see what he was looking at, but I knew he was choking on an obscene amount of numbers as he read the account balance.

"Ah, Mrs Décarie," he stammered. "Charlotte."

"You can call me Mrs Décarie," I obnoxiously corrected.

"This is a sizeable transaction." Garett rose to his feet. "I can't authorise it from here. You're going to have to deal with my manager."

I shrugged as if it was no big deal. "Fine," I replied. "Get him in here. I'll wait."

"I'll wait too," said Lily, finally sounding more like herself. She plucked one of the brochures out of the pile and waved it at him. "Maybe we'll fill out a customer service survey while we wait."

***

Dealing with the bank manager took forever. My care factor when it came to our finances was zero, and after asking me a heap of business related questions that I had no answers for, he realised it too. Finally losing patience with me, he picked up the phone and ordered a teller to draft me a cheque.

"Please have your husband call me at his earliest convenience," he urged on his way out Garett's office. "I'd like to discuss this matter with him personally."

Lily leaned closer. "Are you sure about this, Charli?" she whispered.

"No," I whispered back. "But let's roll with it anyway."

***

As good as it felt to stick it to Garret, victory was fleeting. Not only was Lily still broke, but she'd also been humiliated at the hand of a creepy ghost from her past. I had no idea what sort of history they shared, but I knew it was ugly.

It had been painful to watch, and yet again, I felt responsible. By the time we got in the car, I'd apologised a hundred times.

"It's not your fault, Charli," she muttered.

I briefly glanced at her before pulling out onto the road. "But it was my idea to go."

"You didn't know that was going to happen," she replied. "That guy is a total dick. Always has been."

I was desperate to know how she knew Garret,

but I held off asking. Despite the fact that I'd wedged myself firmly in the middle of it, it really was none of my business.

The journey home was spent in silence. When we rounded the corner of our street, Lily finally spoke up. "I'm never going to be more than I am, Charli."

I slowed the car, focusing more attention on her than the road ahead. "What do you mean, Lil?"

"You said people can change," she replied. "I don't think that's true."

The only thing more worrying than her words was her tone of voice. She sounded flat, dull and broken. I had no idea how to deal with her – or what to say – so I stayed quiet and let her speak.

"No matter how far I remove myself from who I used to be, people refuse to let me forget."

"Oh, Lily," I whispered.

Without warning, she buried her face in her hands and burst into tears. "I can't move forward," she sobbed. "I'm stuck."

Desperate to comfort her, I pulled into my driveway, ripped on the handbrake, and threw my arms around her. "Please, please don't cry," I begged. "Just talk to me."

An eternity had passed before she pulled herself together enough to speak, and when she did, her topic of choice was the smarmy banker. "When I knew him, his name was Garry." She spat out his name with pure venom. "Garret must be his fancy financier name."

"Trust me, Lily," I scoffed. "There's nothing fancy about a man who wears clip-on ties."

She almost laughed but didn't quite get there. "The popular girls in high school used to hang out at the football club in Sorell on Saturday nights," she said. "Do you remember?"

I shook my head, telling her no. "I was never popular," I reminded her. "I used to hang out with Nicole and a packet of Tim Tams."

"You were lucky then."

After a thoughtful pause, the conversation continued, and the more she spoke, the harder it became to listen.

"The players called us the A-girls," she revealed.

I wasn't sure what that meant. "As in A-listers?" I asked naïvely.

"No, Charli." Her voice was tiny. "A as in always. Always up for anything."

I'd spent my awkward teenage years thinking that the popular girls had it all. From the outside looking in, they were confident, happy and admired. Lily wasn't the strongest in that crowd, but she was always destined to have a place because her sister was the queen. What I didn't know was that their entire empire was built on dirt.

"When you're young and desperate for acceptance, you do some appalling things." Every word out of her mouth was laced with shame. "And I was the most desperate of them all." The tissues on her lap had been wrung into a million pieces. She began picking the lint off her skirt. "I grew up being told I was stupid and useless," she whispered. "And that no man would ever want me."

It was logical to assume that the taunts had come from Jasmine, but I'd seen her mother in action first hand. Chances are, it was a team effort.

"I guess I set out to prove them wrong, and for a long time it worked," she explained. "Win, lose, or draw, there was a clubhouse full of blokes on a Saturday night who were only too willing to tell me how pretty and smart I was – for a price."

"I'm so sorry, Lil."

There was absolutely nothing else I could say. I was sorry that her family treated her so poorly, and I was sorrier that she'd allowed men to treat her even worse.

"Don't feel sorry for me," she demanded, pulling in a long steadying breath. "I don't need pity."

"I don't pity you."

"Good," she snapped. "Because I worked it out, right? I grew up, stopped whoring around and ditched the trashy outfits." The sarcastic edge to her voice got lost in pure despair. "I tried to smarten myself up too." She picked up her phone and shook it. "I have a word-of-the-day app for Christ's sake."

The corner of my mouth lifted. "What's today's word?"

Lily swiped her finger across the screen. "In-ex-tric-able," she replied, breaking it into syllables.

"Impossible to disentangle or separate." She let out a humourless snicker. "That's apt, isn't it?"

I nodded, but couldn't bring myself to laugh. I hadn't heard anything funny in hours.

"I disentangled myself from my sister." The words raged out of her. "I did everything right, Charli."

"I know."

"And then Lisa comes back, and she's no better than she was in her A-girl days. She's launching herself at Noah like some sex starved alley cat, and I'm so bloody weak that I can't bring myself to put a stop to it."

I quickly replayed her rant in my head, and still couldn't make sense of it. "You've lost me, Lil."

She lifted her head, staring at me with teary, red eyes. "I've been seeing Noah for months."

"Romantically?" I choked.

"Yes," she replied sadly.

Lily Tate wasn't the first girl in the Cove to keep a relationship under wraps. Gabrielle pioneered that move years ago, but I suspect their motives were wildly different.

"Why are you keeping it a secret?" I gently asked.

Pure agony swept her face. "Because he doesn't know anything beyond the last three months," she whimpered. "Jasmine and her cronies would be champing at the bit to fill him in on all the sordid details that I'm trying to leave behind." She waved her phone at me. "Inextricable, remember?"

"You're not that girl anymore, Lily," I said strongly. "He'll understand."

She rubbed her eyes with the heels of her hands, still trying to pull herself together. "Have you ever felt like you're not good enough, Charli?"

I huffed out a sharp breath. "I have been made to feel unworthy a hundred million times," I told her. "But never by Adam. He only sees the good, even when I show him nothing but bad. If Noah is a keeper, he's only going to see the good."

I folded my arms to stop myself reaching out and shaking her. I'd never been more determined to get a point across in my whole entire life.

"I don't think I can keep him now," she sniffed. "I'm pretty sure it ended today."

"Just talk to him," I muttered, looking across at my house. "Honesty is always the best policy."

Lily let out a tired laugh. "Are you talking about me or you?"

"Me, probably." I reached into my bag and grabbed the gazillion-dollar cheque. "I have to go inside and tell my husband that I spent the afternoon closing all of our bank accounts."

13. CONSTRUCTIVE EDITING

Lily

When the only option you have is to put on a brave face and get on with it, life becomes much easier. In a last ditch effort to recoup some reward for the mass of doggie couture taking up space in my house, I spent the next weekend flogging my wares at the Salamanca markets.

It didn't make me rich, but the feedback was positive and just knowing that a handful of pups were going to be spending winter comfortably decked out in my outfits made me smile.

The next mission when it came to getting on with it was finding a job that didn't entail sweeping hair. Employment options in a small town are limited at the best of times, but when your qualifications are stunted too, it's nearly impossible.

My résumé was hardly stellar. Since leaving school, I'd waitressed at my parents' vineyard restaurant, worked as my sister's salon lackey, and made outfits for pets in my spare time.

I didn't even include the short stint at Alex's café. There's just no easy way to explain that the nicest, most laidback bloke in the Cove cracked after three weeks of working with me. I could still recall his dismissal speech word for word. "I'm sorry, Lil," he said regretfully. "It's not me; it's you. You're going to kill yourself working here."

I couldn't even take offense. Being hit with a ninety degree shot of steam from a coffee machine hurts, and I managed to do it more than once.

With the exception of the Blake's café, I handed my mediocre résumé out to every small business in town. Nothing came of it, and with a heavy soul and a pang of nausea, I made the tough call to contact Jasmine and ask for my job back.

"I think we need a mediator," she foolishly suggested. "We need to set some ground rules before you come back."

It was one of the most ridiculous things I'd

heard in a while, but it was far too early to rock the boat by saying so.

"Meet me at the vineyard in an hour," she instructed. "Dad can oversee the proceedings."

She made it sound as if we were headed to court, but I couldn't deny that having Dad there would make things easier. Unlike my mother, he was impartial and fair. If Jasmine fired up, he wasn't above hosing her down.

***

My family home is a stately farmhouse on the south side of town. It doesn't boast ocean views, but there are worse sights to wake up to than artfully planted rows of grape vines.

The instant I pulled up to the house, I knew my father wasn't there. His white Land Rover was missing and parked in its place was the Davis' ridiculous souped-up minivan.

I wasn't sure if his absence was a last minute change to the program or a deliberate snookering. Either way, I was probably screwed.

My mother met me at the door with a huge hot

pink smile and an uncharacteristic hug. "I knew you'd come to your senses, sweetheart," she crowed. "It's lovely to have both of my daughters back on the same side."

I'd never understood why there had to be sides, but there was no denying that an invisible line existed. As long as I was towing the line, I was walking on the good side, and as much as it pained me, that would be my path from now on.

As soon as I rounded the corner into the dining room, I knew the stage had been set. Lisa and Jasmine sat side-by-side at the table, both doing their best to look superior.

I stopped dead in my tracks, glowering at Lisa. "What are you doing here?" The bitter question raged out of me. "This has nothing to do with you."

"She's our friend, Lil," Jasmine said pointedly.

Lisa's smirk was as black as her heart. "I'm just here for moral support," she replied.

I pulled out a chair and sat opposite my sister. "But you have no morals, Lisa."

Part of me was hoping she'd ask me to explain

myself. Using a real life kitten as a prop to win the affections of the local vet was about as wanton as a woman could be, and I would've gladly told her so.

Civility was slipping fast, but my mother saved the day by waltzing back into the room with a plate of sandwiches and a pot of coffee. "Isn't it lovely to have the whole gang back together again?" she asked.

Jasmine's reaction to the juvenile statement was swift. "We're not a gang, Mum," she corrected with a haughty laugh. "We're just best friends."

A groan of absolute disgust escaped me. "Can we get on with this, please?" I asked. "I've got things to do."

"What things?" asked Lisa. "Packing your bags for fashion week?"

Ordinarily, a bitchy comment like that would've given me palpitations, but as I stared her down from across the table, I realised there was nothing but calm in my heart. I was better than the likes of Lisa Reynolds, and I always had been.

"I'm not going to fashion week," I casually confessed.

"The deal fell through?" The genuine concern in Jasmine's voice threw me. "I'm sorry, Lil."

"There never was a deal," accused Lisa, cackling like a demon. "Charli made it all up."

Mum stopped plating up morning tea, sat down beside me and reached for my hand. "That little wench is a born liar. I'll never understand what that lovely American sees in her."

"Maybe you should ask Mitchell," I dully replied. "He fell for her first."

"Rubbish," scoffed my mother, dropping my hand. "My son would never –"

Surprisingly, Jasmine cut her off. "He did, Mum," she confirmed. "He loved her. Let it go."

Literally squirming in her seat, Lisa threw her two cents in. "She's still a dirty liar," she snapped. "She made poor Lily look stupid."

Mum obviously agreed. She reached across and patted my hand. "Don't worry about it, sweetheart." Her tone was sickly sweet. "You can pick up where you left off at the salon and put this whole nasty episode behind you."

"What about your business?" asked Jasmine.

"Have you completely given up?"

On the off chance that she was genuinely interested, I answered her. "It hasn't taken off as I'd hoped," I confessed. "But I did sell quite a few pieces at the markets last weekend."

I knew my sister inside and out. The smile she gave was true, which made me minutely hopeful that Lisa hadn't completely poisoned her soul. "That's great, Lil," she praised. "I knew people would love them."

"But you have to think long term," said my mother. "Not everyone has the luck of Charli Blake. We can't all enjoy the lifestyle of a kept woman."

She'd been marginally well behaved until that point, but the impending spinster lecture was a sure-fire sign that things were on the downward slide.

"I'm not exactly washed-up yet," I muttered.

"Tell me, Lil," sneered Lisa. "How does one recognise that they've finally become an old maid?"

I felt the smirk that swept my face, and it was

just as wicked as hers. "They buy a kitten," I replied. "That's the end of the line right there."

***

Despite the mild drama, I left the vineyard feeling completely intact. Lisa's best efforts at rattling my cage failed, mainly because I got in first and gave her a good shake instead. It felt a lot like victory, and there was only one person I could think to share it with.

I called Charli from the car and asked if she had time to meet. Neither of us were particularly skilled when it came to being friends, but there was merit in trying. We didn't talk every day – or even every other day – but picking up where we left off was always easy.

"I'm just on my way to the café," she told me. "Can you meet me there?"

"I'm not sure," I vaguely replied. "Your dad gave me a lifetime ban. Do you think it still stands?"

Her warm laugh was contagious. "You'll be fine," she insisted. "I'll vouch for you."

Thankfully, Alex wasn't much of an enforcer. After making me promise not to touch the coffee machine, he agreed to relax the rules. "Can I trust you alone for an hour?" he asked.

The question could only have been for Charli. Alex wouldn't have trusted me alone for a minute.

"Yeah," she replied. "Why?"

He was already reaching for his keys. "Because I promised Gabi I'd take her to lunch last Thursday," he explained. "Today seems like a good day to follow through."

Charli put the back of her hand to her forehead. "My father," she swooned. "The last of the true romantics."

As Alex slipped out the door, she moved to the business side of the counter. "Tea or coffee?"

"Tea, I think."

"Me too," she replied, sounding totally unenthused. "But what I really want is wine."

"Rough day?"

"No." Her smile was wicked. "I'm just in the really unfortunate position of craving wine while knocked up. It starts early in the mornings."

"Really?"

"Yep. By lunch time, I'd just about kill for a chardonnay."

It felt good to laugh, and I realised that it happened most often when I was around her. "We wasted a lot of time being enemies, didn't we?" I asked, thinking out loud.

Charli smiled at the random question, though it had a rueful tinge. "I try not to live with regrets, Lil," she replied. "Life is too short."

"I have a few." I ran my finger along the grain of the wooden counter. "But I'm learning to live with them."

"Attagirl," she encouraged. "And because you're doing so well, I'll let you decide which cake we're going to steal." She stepped to the side, showcasing the fridge section of the counter with a swipe of her hands.

"You're going to get me banned again."

"If Alex didn't want us to eat cake, he would've taken them with him," she reasoned.

There was just no arguing with that kind of logic. "Mud cake," I decided, tapping my finger on the glass.

Momentarily dropping from view, Charli leaned into the fridge and grabbed the huge cake. "Excellent choice," she praised, thudding it down on the counter.

I stepped off the stool. "I'll get a knife," I offered.

"No knife." Her serious tone stopped me dead in my tracks. "Just get two forks."

There wasn't a number high enough to describe the amount of calories we consumed over the next half hour, and if I hadn't confiscated Charli's fork, she might've polished off the whole cake. "Where do you put it all?" I asked incredulously.

"Hopefully it all goes to him." She patted her little potbelly. "And not on my hips like last time."

I smiled at her. "You think it's a boy?"

She shrugged. "Just a hunch."

"A little Adam would be so freaking cute."

"Speaking of cute," she drawled. "I ran into Noah in town the other day. He asked about you."

The mention of his name sent a small jolt of sorrow through me. We hadn't spoken in days.

Nancy's routine injection appointment the week before had been exactly that – routine. There was no flirty banter and no stolen kiss at the end of it. We were over, and I felt like I'd been robbed of something precious.

"I really screwed things up." Unable to look at it anymore, I pushed the cake carcass further away. "Noah Holt is the one regret I *am* having trouble living with. I hate the way it ended."

A glint of pity flashed in her brown eyes. "Do you miss him?"

"What sort of question is that, Charlotte?"

"An important one, Lilian," she huffed.

I didn't try stopping her when she reached for her fork. I was too busy mulling over her question. "Yes, I miss him," I said finally.

She violently stabbed her fork into the cake as if she as trying to kill it. "Why?"

"Charli, are you just grasping for conversation?" I glowered at her. "Because if you are, we can talk about the weather or something."

"No, I'm serious," she replied, picking a shard of chocolate off her fork. "I want to know."

I spent a long moment really thinking things through. I couldn't claim to love a man that I was just getting to know, but like wasn't a strong enough word. I liked Noah, but I liked the chocolate cake we'd just devoured too.

Then it finally hit me, and the real reason I missed him flew out of my mouth like a shot from a gun. "I like who I am when he's around."

Charli leaned closer, pointing her fork at me. "And that, my friend, is exactly why you should've fought harder to keep it together. He might be the one who's minding your shadow."

Total confusion set in. "Charli, be honest," I urged. "You gave in to the chardonnay this morning, didn't you?"

"No." She chuckled. "Shadow minding is a legitimate job, I promise."

I swatted my napkin down on the table. "You're crazy."

"You might be right," she agreed, leaning in close again. "But crazy people weave lovely tales, and I have a doozy for you if you're interested." Of course I was bloody interested. The creepy tone she'd adopted made it impossible not to be. "It's about a girl called Tayana," she began. "She was Finnish."

"Finished already?" I teased. "That was quick."

"Finnish from Finland, smart-arse." She pulled a face at me. "Tayana was beautiful, but she had a really hard life working in a restaurant that was owned by the meanest fairies in the land."

"I didn't know fairies could be mean."

"I'll bet you didn't know they could run restaurants either."

I dropped my head, chuckling down at the table. "No, I guess not."

"Anyway," she continued, pretending to straighten the cutlery. "The ghastly fairies who worked in the kitchen were particularly cruel, and they made Tayana's life a misery."

"If you tell me they made her sweep hair, I'm out of here."

She brought her mug of tea to her lips. "Worse," she replied, taking a sip. "They beat her black and blue."

I slumped back in my chair. "Jesus, Charli," I

grumbled. "What happened to weaving lovely words?"

She answered with a shrug of her shoulders. "The vicious fairies were intent on destroying her, and they soon figured out a way to do it using their magic."

In the space of just a few minutes, Charli managed to blow everything I knew about fairies to smithereens. It was terrifying and fascinating all at the same time.

"Have you told Bridget this story?" I asked curiously.

"I would if I had to."

I wondered what that meant, but didn't dare ask. "Keep going," I prompted.

"Well, because of a magic spell, every time they whacked her, a piece of her soul chipped away and fell to the floor." Her tone was as dire as the story. "Before long, everything that made Tayana lovely and special was laying on the floor – courage, optimism, self-worth, creativity, strength – her entire soul."

I was starting to feel choked up but wasn't sure

why. I swallowed hard, reminding myself that it was just a silly story.

"Once they were sure they'd knocked all the pieces of goodness and light out of her, the meanest fairy of them all stepped in."

"Please don't make it worse," I whispered.

"Her name was Banu," she said, ignoring me. "So while the other fairies held the poor girl down, Banu kicked all of the pieces into a pile and wrapped them up in Tayana's shadow."

For someone who'd grown up imagining fairies to be spritely little beings caked in glitter, the story was an education and a half. Not only were the fairies evil, but they were also proficient travellers. According to Charli, Banu took off to Poland with Tayana's shadow and chucked it in an icy river.

"Bastards," I grumbled sourly.

"What they didn't know at the time was that someone saw them hurl it into the water – a boy – a Polish boy called Stanislaus." She announced his name with reverence, but I couldn't shake the feeling that she'd made it up on the spot.

"He was cute, right?" I asked hopefully. "Please

make Stan cute."

I couldn't explain why it mattered, but it did.

"I'm not making this up, Lil." She put her hand to her heart. "But for the record, yes, he was extremely handsome."

I actually breathed a sigh of relief. "Excellent news," I replied. "Feel free to continue."

"Thank you." She dipped her head. "As soon as Banu left, Stan jumped in and rescued the shadow from the water. When he took a peek and saw what was inside, he made it his mission to find Tayana and return her missing pieces."

"How did he know that –"

"He just did, Lil," she interrupted. "It's magic. You just have to go with it."

"Okay." I threw both hands up in surrender. "I'm going with it."

"Poor Tayana was lost without her pieces," said Charli. "The cuts and bruises eventually healed so she was beautiful again on the outside, but her soul was empty – totally void of the good kind of beauty."

"That's so freaking sad," I lamented.

"She wandered the earth without purpose or joy for years." Charli held one finger up. "But then one day, something amazing happened."

I crossed my fingers, making her smile. "Stan found her?"

"He sure did," she said smugly. "And as soon as he returned her shadow, Tayana became whole again – confident, happy and brave – and it was all thanks to the lovely Stan."

For a short minute, the ending was perfect, but then Charli added a footnote.

"Banu is still at it, you know," she said gravely. "She's everywhere. And to this day, all over the world, lovely kind-hearted boys are two steps behind her picking up the shadows of beautiful girls with missing pieces."

It was impossible to hear a story like that and remain unaffected. I'd spent the vast majority of my life feeling inadequate, and I couldn't help wondering if it was because I was missing a few vital pieces.

If I was in for a penny, I had to be in for a pound. I let my mind wander as I considered whether Tayana's story applied to me. Before meeting Noah, I had zero confidence and a serious lack of self-esteem. I wasn't exactly brimming with those traits now, but I was getting better.

Without his encouragement, I would never have broken free of Jasmine and gone out on my own. And despite the fact that Pawesome Designs had been an epic failure, I still found the courage to try because he was on the sidelines cheering me on.

"Do you think Noah might be holding my shadow?"

There was no holding the ridiculous question back, but Charli didn't seem too perturbed by it.

She shrugged. "I don't know, Lilian."

"Well, what do you think happens when your shadow is returned?"

Charli took another sip of tea and then turned the question back to me. "What do you think happens?"

I stared at her for a long time, deliberating. "I have no idea," I had to admit. "But I hope it involves balloons and ribbons and puppies and champagne." I rose to my feet and grabbed my bag. "I have to be somewhere, Charli."

"I figured as much," she replied, smiling. "Say hi to Noah for me."

***

The city vet lived on a five-acre property on the north side of town, and because I was desperate to see him, it took forever to get there.

Too much thinking time is never good when you're anticipating a frosty reception, and by the time I pulled up at the house, it took all I had not to turn around and go home.

Besides my nerves, the biggest obstacle I had to overcome before knocking on the door was Hank, who was sprawled out on the doormat.

I leaned over him and knocked but got no answer, and I could feel the icicles forming because of it.

"This is a bad idea," I mumbled, nudging Hank with my foot.

Honey was a little more welcoming than her comatose buddy, enthusiastically wagging her tail as I stepped off the porch, but she made no attempt to follow me.

Knowing Noah had animals to tend to, I decided to venture a little bit further before calling the mission off. I kept my distance as I passed the pigpen. Two of the slovenliest hogs I'd ever seen were flat out in the dirt. Neither paid me a skerrick of attention, but they still looked shady as heck.

I passed another pen that looked empty, but when Honey came bounding over to me, I knew Noah had to be close by. Over the impromptu game of hide-and-seek, I called out his name.

"I'm over here," came a distant reply.

At a total loss, I turned my head in every direction before looking down at the friendly Cocker Spaniel at my feet. "Honey, pretend you're Lassie," I told her. "Take me to your leader."

"I think you're confusing Lassie with an alien," said a voice from behind.

Almost tripping on Honey, I spun around to find Noah standing right in front of me.

"She's a smart dog." I could feel my cheeks burning. "She would've figured it out."

He dropped his head, unsuccessfully hiding his smile. "She is the smart one," he agreed. "Hank is as dumb as a box of rocks."

My eyes drifted to the house. Hank was still fast asleep. "Not much of a watchdog either," I added.

Noah smiled again, but didn't speak, which paved the way for unease.

"I went to the clinic first," I stammered. "Susie said you'd left for the day."

He nodded. "I wanted to check on the kids."

"*Your* kids?" It was hard not to sound horrified by the notion, but I think I pulled it off.

"Sort of," he replied. "Come and meet them if you want to."

Considering that he was already walking away when he made the offer, I didn't feel like I had much of a choice. I followed Noah past the pigs and down to a penned area that was shaded by a big oak tree.

A fat nanny goat was tied to the fence, and two baby kids were desperately trying to feed off her. The tiny chocolate brown goats were cuter than any human baby I'd ever seen in my lifetime.

"I'm in love," I announced, leaning on the fence to get a closer look. "How old are they?"

"Four days," he replied. "Cute, aren't they?"

"Yes." I couldn't tear my eyes off them. "But why is their mum tied up?"

After all the poor mama had been through, tethering her to the fence seemed mighty cruel.

"It's temporary," he assured me. "She's not taken kindly to one of the babies. I'm just trying to hold her in place so she can get a feed."

I studied the little family's dynamics closely, and in less than a minute, I realised what he meant. The crotchety goat only had eyes for one of her kids. When the smaller of the two tried to nurse, she butted her away.

Noah jumped the fence and tried to help her get closer, but the mama was having none of it.

"What'll happen if she won't let her eat?" Deep down I already knew the answer, but hearing it out loud still crushed me.

"She'd eventually starve," he replied, wandering back toward me. "But I won't let it get that far."

My eyes drifted back to the goats, and a few

seconds later, I witnessed the worst thing I'd ever seen in my life. When the little goat moved closer to its mother, she kicked her back legs and shunted her into the dirt.

The only thing louder than my horrified scream was the horrible pained bleating of the injured little kid. Noah ran over and snatched her up, and with Honey and me in hot pursuit, rushed her to the house.

Hank wasn't remotely concerned by the medical emergency playing out in front of him. The lazy Lab barely opened his eyes as Noah gave him a nudge and ordered him to get out of the way of the door.

By the time he did finally move, the distraught baby kid was inconsolable. The bleating was deafening and impossibly hard to listen to. I was sobbing, unable to pull myself together enough to speak, but Noah was as calm as ever.

He grabbed a blanket off the couch as he passed, and set the little goat down on the living room floor.

"You're alright, little girl," he soothed, checking her over.

"She has blood on her ear," I cried.

"Her mum gave her a bit of a nip." He leaned, taking a closer look. "She'll be okay."

"Why would she do that?" I was appalled, and scared, and my voice shook because of it. "How could she be so vicious?"

"It happens, Lil," he said casually. "We'll just have to take care of her for a while."

I didn't know the first thing about taking care of a baby goat, and at that moment, I wasn't sure that it would get that far. The poor little kid was shaking like a leaf and still bleating bloody murder.

I stumbled toward the door, desperate to get out of there. "I need some air."

I pulled the door closed behind me, stepped over Hank and made my way down the front steps. If I could've pulled myself together enough to put the keys in the ignition, I would've got in my car and left. Instead, I pulled in a few steadying breaths and headed back to the goat pen.

The mama goat was right where we left her, tied to the fence and casually grazing as if nothing was out of the ordinary. Her other kid stood close to her side, looking as happy and content as a goat could.

I was unreasonably furious with her – so furious that I considered Googling goat curry recipes.

"What's wrong with you?" I growled through the fence. "Why don't you love both of your babies?"

Predictably, she didn't answer me.

"You got it wrong, Nanny goat," I taunted. "That kid is special, and you just gave her the boot."

I turned my attention to the favourite goat. "And you can wipe that smug look off your face," I told him. "You're not such a bigshot."

Honey suddenly appeared, brushing herself against my leg as if she was carrying out some sort of doggie welfare check. "It's okay, Honey." I gave her a pat. "I'm not crazy."

At least, I didn't think I was. Taking my frustration out on oblivious farm animals wasn't exactly the norm, but it felt wonderful.

At that moment, the tiny reject goat was my soul sister. I knew exactly how it felt to be shunted from the fold. I also knew from firsthand experience that there was no one better to pick up her pieces than the caring, compassionate city vet.

***

When I finally pulled myself together and returned to the house, things were much calmer. The bleating had stopped, and the little goat was on the floor, sitting comfortably on the blanket beside Noah.

"Do you think she'll be okay?" I asked in a small voice.

"She should be," he said, looking up at me. "We'll just have to take care of her ourselves for a while."

I wandered over to him and knelt down on the floor. "I don't have a clue how to look after her."

"I'll show you," he offered.

It was a dizzying shift. An hour earlier, we were barely talking. Now we were discussing co-parenting a reject baby goat.

I reached, cautiously stroking my hand across her dark brown fur. "I came here to talk." I glanced at him. "I wanted to apologise."

"You've nothing to be sorry for, Lil."

I believed he meant it, but he was wrong.

"I didn't handle things well," I told him. "And because of that, I'm not sure where we stand."

"How about we just start at the beginning?" he said simply.

I lifted my head. "A do over?"

His shoulders lifted. "If that's what you want to call it."

"What would you call it?"

"Constructive editing," he replied, smiling.

A flutter of hope filtered through my heart. He was right; there was no need to start over. We just needed to iron out a few kinks, and thanks to the insight of my crazy knocked up friend, I felt strong enough to do it.

"Things are already different, Noah."

"They are," he agreed, reaching to pat the baby goat to his left. "We have a kid now."

***

Caring for a baby goat is as demanding as caring for a newborn human. Probably inspired by Patty the lush, Noah made the kid a bed by lining a laundry basket with a soft blanket. He lit the living room fire to keep her extra warm, and after handfeeding her from a baby's bottle, he tucked her into her basket.

"She needs a name." Noah flopped down beside me on the couch, probably exhausted. "We can't keep calling her kid."

I rested my head on his shoulder. "Why do you like animals so much?"

If he thought the random question was odd, he didn't let on. "They're not as complicated as people," he replied, tangling his fingers through mine. "I'm as simple as they are so we connect well."

I let out a soft laugh. "I'm simple too."

He put his hand on my chin, tilting my head. "You're not, Lil." His green eyes locked on mine. "You're creative and passionate and resilient. A girl with those traits is far from simple."

"You see that in me?" My shaky voice was barely there.

His hand slipped through the buttons of my

shirt, resting on my heart. "I can feel it in you," he said in a deliciously low tone. "Don't sell yourself short."

Twisting in his hold, I threw my arms around him and kissed him to within an inch of his life, overcome by nothing more than the pure joy of knowing that he was the one who'd eventually make me whole.

Finally, I broke the kiss. "Penny," I whispered, inching his head back so I could see his eyes. "We should call her Penny."

Noah leaned, brushing his lips against mine. "Perfect," he murmured.

It was perfect. If I was in for a penny, I was in for a pound.

14. FANFARE

Charli

All good things come to those who wait, and Lily had been waiting a lifetime.

Returning to her job at the salon must've been impossibly hard, but in true Lily style, she did it without making a fuss.

From what I could tell, nothing had changed. Jasmine was still a tyrant, and Lily's long work days were spent sweeping up and making coffee because of it.

I asked her more than once how she coped, and her answer never changed. "I just have to be patient," she replied. "Better things are coming my way, Charli."

Little did she know, her patience had paid off.

After spending two months tirelessly pitching the story of Pawesome Designs to her editors, Bente was finally given the green light.

Lily had no idea that she'd made page three of the Manhattan Tribune. She also had no clue that she'd made hundreds of sales in the five days since the article had gone to print, but that was about to change.

Making a song and dance had never been my forte, but news like this deserved all the fanfare I could muster.

Following my instructions to a T, Noah met us a few doors down from the salon with Penny the goat in tow.

At first, he was on board with my plan, but while I put the finishing touches to the big reveal, he was having second thoughts.

"Are you sure this isn't overkill?" he asked, sounding worried.

It was a fair question. The bottle of champagne I handed him was a traditional celebratory gift, but the huge bunch of balloons that I'd tied to it was somewhat excessive.

"It's lovely overkill, Noah," chimed Bridget, skipping over cracks in the pavement. "It's Lily's happy day."

"She'll love it," I added.

"You wouldn't steer me wrong, would you, Charli?" He looked up at the mass of coloured balloons floating above his head. "This is way over the top."

I grabbed him by the shoulders and gave him a shake. "An article in the Manhattan Tribune is worth celebrating," I replied. "This is going to be huge."

Noah didn't look convinced, so I tried harder. "I checked the website again before we left home," I told him.

"And?"

"Over six hundred sales!" I slapped his arm. "She's killing it."

"Overkilling it," added Bridget seriously.

Noah's eyes darted between us. "You two work as a tag team. You realise that, right?"

I slipped Penny's leash off my wrist and handed it to him. "Shut up and take your goat,"

I replied, laughing.

"This is so shady," he mumbled.

I couldn't blame him for being distrustful. Even though the news of their romance was well and truly busted, Lily fought hard to keep it private and low key. Sending her city vet beau into the salon armed with a bunch of balloons, a bottle of Moët and a goat was anything but low key.

"This is Lily's ultimate celebration kit," I explained. "Balloons, ribbons, champagne and a puppy."

His line of sight dropped to the chocolate brown goat at his feet. "Penny's not a puppy."

I pulled a copy of the Tribune out of my bag and slapped it against his chest. "She is today."

Seriously close to being overloaded, Noah slipped the newspaper under his arm. "This is about more than the article, isn't it?" he asked.

"Yes," I said simply.

A confused frown swept his handsome face. "What am I missing, Charli?"

I reached up and straightened the collar on

his shirt. "Nothing is missing, Noah," I quietly replied. "And because of that, Lily Tate is now a hundred percent whole."

The End

Stone Roses
(Book Seven, The Wishes Series)

No one ever looks for cracks in perfection, and Adam Décarie is no exception.

He loves his wife and he loves his children. As far as he's concerned, he doesn't have a problem in the world.

After a difficult stint in New York, Adam, Charli and Bridget settled back into their free-range life on the beaches of Pipers Cove with ease.

Every day is a joy, and when their precious new baby arrives, everything is perfect.

Adam feels content, blessed and happy.

But Charli feels nothing at all.

And that's a problem.